ALL THE LONG YEARS
Western Stories

Other Five Star Titles
Edited by Bill Pronzini:

Under the Burning Sun: Western Stories by H.A. DeRosso
Renegade River: Western Stories by Giff Cheshire
Riders of the Shadowlands: Western Stories by H.A. DeRosso
Heading West: Western Stories by Noel M. Loomis

ALL THE LONG YEARS
Western Stories

Bill Pronzini

Five Star
Unity, Maine

Five Star First Edition Western Series.

First Edition, Second Printing.

Published in 2001 in conjunction with
Golden West Literary Agency.

Set in 11 pt. Plantin by Al Chase.

Printed in the United States on permanent paper.

Library of Congress Cataloging-in-Publication Data

Pronzini, Bill.
    All the long years : western stories / by Bill Pronzini. —
1st ed.
      p.   cm.
    "Five Star western."
    ISBN 0-7862-2118-6 (hc : alk. paper)
    I. Title.
PS3566.R67 A78 2001
813'.54—dc21
                                       00-057804

Contents

Foreword

The stories in this collection span thirty years of Western fiction writing and encompass a variety of characters, settings, and themes. They are peopled by such familiar figures as lawmen, ranchers, cowhands, gamblers, detectives, newspapermen, and timber jacks, and by such little used individuals as stable hands, bartenders, saddle-makers, tramp printers, traveling dentists, moonshiners, and patent medicine drummers. Settings extend from small, mythical Montana towns to actual locales: the California Mother Lode, the Oregon wilderness, Death Valley. In scope they run the gamut from grim character studies to tales of action and mystery to farcical humor.

The earliest, "Decision," first published in 1971, shares a similar theme—the drifter in search of roots and commitment who encounters a woman in distress—with one of the most recent, "Engines," first published in 1997. The former is Western myth, the latter contemporary and grounded in fact, and the resolution to each is completely different. Other selections are also variations on classic Western themes. "All the Long Years," a tale of wrong choices and bitter loss, begins with the brand blotting of a wealthy rancher's cattle by the angry son of a neighbor. The hardships faced by a deep-woods logging gang, the fitting vengeance they exact on a tyrannical leader, and "the damnedest sight a man ever set eyes on" is the stuff of "McIntosh's Chute." Three stories, "Hero," "Markers," and "Fear," deal in diverse ways with the long-range effects of acts of violence and cowardice. "Lady One-Eye" is a Western mystery hybrid featuring 1890s

San Francisco detectives Sabina Carpenter and John Quincannon—whose other adventures can be found in the novels, QUINCANNON (Walker, 1985), BEYOND THE GRAVE (Walker, 1986) written with Marcia Muller, and the collection, CARPENTER AND QUINCANNON, PROFESSIONAL DETECTIVE SERVICES (Crippen & Landru, 1998).

The remaining entries are less easily categorized. " 'Give-A-Damn' Jones" champions the life and times of a 19th-Century tramp printer, and tells how a brief encounter with one such "hand-pegger" alters the entire shape of a young man's life. "The Gambler" examines nearly fifty years of professional gambling in the Old West in a stylistically unconventional fashion. "Doc Christmas, Painless Dentist" and "Wooden Indian" are ironic and light-hearted tales, respectively, of an amazing extraction made by a shrewd traveling charlatan and of a band of native Americans and their remarkable chief. "Fyfe and the Drummers" and "Not a Lick of Sense" are humorous short-shorts that might be classified as Western tall tales.

Some critics would have us believe that the traditional Western story is limited to conventional plots, stock characters, and simplistic themes. This is patently not the case. The Western tale can be and is many things. I hope the fourteen stories gathered here demonstrate this fact, although they represent only a fraction of the broad range of possibilities.

Bill Pronzini
Petaluma, California

All the Long Years

I caught him some past noon on the second day, over on the west edge of my range near Little Creek. Thing was, he wasn't much of a cow thief. He'd come onto my land in broad daylight, bold as brass, instead of night herding and then doing his brand burning elsewhere. And he'd built his fire in a shallow coulée, as if that would keep the smoke from drifting high and far. You could hear the bawling of the cattle a long way off, too.

I picketed my horse in some brush and eased up to the rim of the coulée and hunkered down behind a chokecherry to have a look at him. I wanted him to be a stranger, or one of the small dirt ranchers from out beyond the Knob. But you don't always get what you want in this life—hell, no, you don't— and I didn't this time. He wasn't a drifter, and he wasn't a dirt rancher. He was just who I figured the brand blotter to be: young Cal Dennison.

He had a running iron heating in the fire, and he was squatting alongside, smoking a quirly while he waited. Close by were a lean-shanked orange dun cow pony and two of my Four Dot cows that he'd hobbled with piggin' strings. The cows were both young brindle heifers, good breeding stock.

The tip of the running iron was starting to turn red. Cal Dennison rotated it once, finished his smoke, and went to drag one of the heifers over near the fire. When he set to work with that iron, he had his back to where I was. The smell of singed hair came up sharp on the warm afternoon breeze.

I stood and drew my Colt six-gun. Off on my left there was an easy path into the coulée. I moved there and made my way

down, slow and careful. The bawling of the heifers covered
what sounds I made. I stopped a dozen paces behind and to
one side of him, close enough to see that he was almost done
turning my Four Dot brand into a solid bar. If I gave him
enough time, he'd burn a D above the bar, the way he had
with other of my cows over the past week or so. Then he'd do
the other heifer and afterwards herd both over onto D-Bar
graze, next to mine on the other side of Little Creek. D-Bar
was Lyle Dennison's brand.

But I didn't give him enough time. I put the Colt's
hammer on cock and said fast and loud: "You're caught, boy.
Set still where you are."

He must have heard the *sicking* of the hammer because he was
already moving by the time I got the words out. Cat-quick, he
came all the way around with a look of wild surprise on his face.

"I said set still! You want to die, boy?"

Sight of the Colt and the tone of my voice, if not the words
themselves, finally froze him on one knee with the running
iron still in his hand. I could have emptied the Colt into him
by the time he dropped the iron and drew his own sidearm,
and he knew it. I watched him wet his mouth, get hold of himself, watched the wildness smooth out into an expression of
sullen defiance.

"Bennett," he said, the way most men would say:
"Horseshit."

"Put the iron down. Slow."

He did it.

"Now your six-gun, even slower. Just two fingers."

He did that, too.

"Untie the heifer. Then go do the same with the other
one."

It took him a minute or so to get the piggin' strings off the
first heifer's legs. She scrambled up and went loping away

down the coulée, still bawling. He got the second cow untied in quicker time, and, while that one ran off, he stood hipshot, glaring at me. I'd seen him in Cricklewood a few times, but the Dennisons and the Bennetts had kept their distance these past twenty years; this was the first I'd had a good look at the boy up close. He'd be past nineteen now. Tall and sinewy and fair-skinned—the image of his ma, I thought. Same light brown curls and dark smoky eyes and proud stance. How long had Ellen Dennison been dead? Ten years? Eleven? Funny how time distorts your sense of its passage, how single years among all the long years blend and blur together until you can't tell one from another.

"Well!" young Cal said. "Now what?"

I didn't answer him. Instead, I moved over to where he'd been by the fire and kicked his sidearm, an old Allen & Wheelock Navy .36, in among the branches of a wild rose bush.

He said angrily: "What'd you do that for? Them thorns'll scratch hell out of it."

"You won't be using it again."

"You going to shoot me, Bennett?"

"Mister Bennett to you."

"Go to hell, *Mister* Bennett."

"This was twenty years ago . . . I'd have already shot you."

"Well, it ain't twenty years ago."

"Rustling can still get you hung in this county."

"I ain't afraid of that. Or you, *Mister* Bennett."

"Then you're a damn' fool in more ways than one."

He tried to work his mouth up into a sneer, but he couldn't quite bring it off. He wasn't near so tough or fearless as he was trying to make out. His gaze shifted away from me, roved up along the rim of the coulée. "Where's the rest of your crew?"

"There's just me. I don't need a crew to run down one

11

punk brand blotter. Only took me a day and a half."

He had nothing to say to that.

I said: "How many of my cows have you burned?"

"You're so god-damn' smart, you figure it out."

"My riders say at least half a dozen."

"Two thousand," he said, smart-mouth.

"All right, then. Your pa know what you been up to?"

". . . No."

"I didn't think so. Whatever else Lyle Dennison is, he's not a brand burner and a cow thief."

"I'll tell you what he is," the boy said. "He's twice the man you are."

"Maybe so. But you're not half the man either of us ever was."

That flared up his anger again. "You stole three thousand acres that belonged to him! You turned him into a broken-down dirt rancher!"

"No. That land belonged to me. Circuit judge said so in open court. . . ."

"You bought that judge! You bribed him! That's always been your way, *Mister* Bennett. Get what you want any way you can . . . lie and steal and cheat to get it. Ain't that right?"

There was another lie on my tongue, but it tasted bitter, and I didn't say it. What did he know about how it was in the old days, a kid like him? Those three thousand acres were mine by right of first possession; my cattle were on free range before Lyle Dennison and others like him showed up in this valley. A man has to fight for what belongs to him, even if it means fighting dirty. If he doesn't, he loses it—and, once it's gone, he'll never get it back. It's gone for good.

"That's what this brand-blotting business is all about?" I asked him. "Something that happened between your pa and me twenty years ago?"

"Damn' right that's what it's all about. Way I figure it, I got as much right to steal your cattle as you had to steal my pa's land."

"Twenty years is a long time, boy. More years than you been on this earth."

"That don't change the way it was. Pa never would do nothing about it . . . he just gave up. But not me. It's my fight now, and I ain't giving up until it's settled, one way or another."

"Why is it your fight now?"

"Because it is."

"Something happen to your pa?"

"That's none of your look-out."

"You've made it my look-out. He didn't pass on, did he?"

"Might as well have."

"Sick, then? Some kind of ailment?"

The boy was silent for a time. But I could see it eating at him, the pain, and the rage and the hate; he had to let it come out or bust with it. When he did let it come, he threw the words at me as if they were knives. "He had a stroke last week. Crippled him. He can't hardly move, can't hardly talk, just lies there in his bed. You satisfied now? That make you happy?"

"No, boy, it doesn't. I'm sorry."

"Sorry? Christ . . . sorry! You son-of-a-bitch. . . ."

"That's enough. Go get your horse."

"What?"

"Get your horse. Lead him up to where mine is picketed."

"You takin' me to town?"

"We're going to the D-Bar. I want to see your pa."

"No!"

"You don't have a say in it. Do what I told you."

"Why? You aim to tell him about this?"

13

"Maybe. Maybe not."

"You do and it'll kill him."

"You should have thought of that before you came onto my land with that running iron."

"I won't go."

"You'll go," I said. "Sitting your saddle or tied across it with a bullet in your leg, either way."

He didn't move until I waggled the Colt at him. Then he spat hard into the grass and swung around and stomped over to where the orange dun was picketed.

Following him and the horse up to the coulée rim, I tried to figure what had put the notion to do this in my head. It wasn't just the brand blotting. And it wasn't because I wanted to mortify the boy in front of Lyle, or that I wanted to pour salt in old wounds. Could be I would tell Lyle about the rustling, but more likely I wouldn't. Maybe it was because Lyle Dennison and me had been friends once, and now he was ailing, likely dying. Maybe it was that young Cal needed to be taught some kind of lesson. Or maybe it was just that there was a crazy need in me to touch the past again.

A man doesn't always know why he does a thing. Or need to know, for that matter. It's just something he has to do, so he goes ahead and does it. Let it go at that.

It was mid-afternoon when we came in sight of the D-Bar ranch buildings. They were grouped in a hollow where Little Creek ran, with the gaunt, snow-rimmed shapes of the Rockies rising up in the distance. I'd expected changes after so many years but none like the ones I saw as we topped the hill above the creek. The place appeared run-down, withered, as if nobody lived there any more. Gaps in the walls of the hip-roofed barn, missing rails in the corral fence, a rusty-wire chicken coop where the bunkhouse had once stood. The main house needed whitewash and new siding and a new roof. There had been flower beds and a vegetable garden once. Now there were a few dried-up vines and bushes here and there, like scattered bones in a graveyard.

Cal said—"You like what you see, *Mister* Bennett?"—and I come to realize he'd been watching me take it all in. It was the first he'd spoken since we had left my land.

"Why haven't you and your pa kept things up?"

"Why? Why the hell you think? He's old, and I ain't got but two hands, and there ain't but twenty-four hours in a day."

"Nobody working for you?"

"Not since anthrax took most of our cows two years ago."

"Anthrax took some of my cows, too," I said.

"Sure it did. But then you went right out and bought some more, didn't you?"

We rode the rest of the way in a new silence. The boy leaned down and pulled the wooden pin that held the sagging gates shut, and we went on across the yard. Even the grass that grew here, even the big shade cottonwoods behind the house and the willows along the creek, seemed to have a dusty, lifeless look.

We drew rein at the tie rail near the house and got down. I said then: "I'll see him alone."

"Hell you will! You go waltzin' in there like you owned the place, he'll have another stroke. . . ."

"You got no say in this, boy. I told you that."

"You can't just bust in on him!"

"I'll announce myself first."

"What about me? You expect me to just stand here and wait for you?"

"That's just what I expect. You won't run. And you won't try fighting me, neither, not with your pa lying in there."

15

We locked gazes. There was as much heat in it as a couple of maverick steers locking horns. But I was older and tougher, and I had a six-gun besides, holstered though it was now and had been for most of the ride. Cal knew it as well as I did. It was what made him look away first, hating himself for doing it and hating me all the harder for backing him down.

He said thickly: "You goin' to tell him?"

"Still haven't made up my mind."

"He'll call you a liar if you do."

I said—"Stand here where you can hear me if I call you."—and went on up the stairs to the screen door. He didn't try to follow me. When I turned to glance back at him, he was rooted to the same spot with the hate shining out of his eyes like light shining out of a red-eye lantern.

I opened the screen door—the inside door was already open—and called: "Lyle? It's Sam Bennett. I've come to talk."

No answer.

"Sing out if you object to my coming in."

Still no answer.

I moved inside, let the screen door bang shut behind me. The day's warmth lay thick in the parlor. Dust, too—a thin layer of it on the floor and on the old, worn furniture. Ellen Dennison had been a neat, clean woman; she would have kept house the same way. But she was long gone. For ten or eleven years now it had been just Lyle and the boy.

"Lyle?"

My voice seemed to come bouncing back at me off the walls. I walked across the room, into a hall with three doors opening off of it. He was beyond the last of them, in the back bedroom. Lying in a four-poster with an old patchwork quilt draped over him. His eyes were wide open. One look at them that way and I knew he was dead.

16

One thin, veined hand lay palm up on the quilt. I went over and touched it, and it was cool and stiff. The stiffness was in his face and body, too. Dead a while, since sometime this morning.

For a time I stood looking down at him. We were the same age, forty-six, but the years had ravaged him where they had only eroded me some. His hair was thin and gray-white, there were lines in his face as deep as cracks in sun-dried mud, and his hands were the hands of a man in his sixties. Death, for him, had come as something of a mercy.

A sadness built in me, seeing him up close like this, newly passed on. I'd never hated Lyle Dennison. He had been my friend once, and then he'd been my enemy, but I had never hated or even disliked him much. I'd hardly thought about him at all after the court fight. Hell, why should I? I'd claimed the three thousand acres, and they were what counted. Land and money and power were the only things that counted.

That was the way I'd thought back then and most of my life, anyhow. It wasn't the way I thought now.

I leaned down to close Lyle's eyes. Then I made my way back through the house and out onto the porch. Cal was standing where I'd left him. The only thing he'd done was to take out the makings and build himself a smoke.

He said around the quirly: "That was some short talk."

"He's dead, Cal," I said.

"What?"

"Your pa is dead. Passed away this morning sometime, looks like."

"You're a god-damn' liar!"

"Go in and see for yourself."

The cigarette dropped out of his mouth, hit the front of his hickory shirt, and showered sparks on the way to the ground. He didn't notice. His face had gone bloodless. "You told him

17

about me. You told him, and he had another stroke. . . ."

"He had another stroke, right enough. But he's been gone for hours. Go on, boy. See for yourself."

He bolted for the stairs. I got out of the way as he ran up and yanked open the screen door and bulled inside. When the door banged shut again, I walked on down to the rail and made a cigarette of my own. But it tasted bad, like I was sucking in sulphur smoke. I threw it away after two drags. Then I just stood there and watched a hawk glide above the cottonwoods along the creek, and waited.

It was close to ten minutes before Cal came back out. By then he had himself under a tight rein, likely so I wouldn't see how much he was grieving. He came down to where I was and looked at me for a space, with the hate in his eyes banked now, smoldering.

He said: "Something I want to know."

"Ask it."

"If he'd been alive, would you've told him?"

"No," I said.

"How come?"

"This business is between you and me. You said as much yourself, back in the coulée."

He seemed to understand, or thought he did. He nodded once. "I'm goin' into town now, talk to the preacher and the undertaker. You can tell Sheriff Gaiters I'll be one place or the other when he wants me."

"What makes you think I'll be talking to Sheriff Gaiters?"

That surprised him some. "Mean you won't?"

"Not this time. But you stay off my land from now on. I catch you there again, or find out about any more brand blotting, you'll pay and pay dear. You hear me?"

"I hear you," he said. "But you better hear something, too, *Mister* Bennett. This don't change nothing. Nothing at all."

18

"I didn't expect it would."

"Just so you know. I ain't my pa's son. I ain't givin' up the way he did, never mind what you say or do."

He turned on his heel and walked over to the corral fence. Stood there with his back to me, gazing out at the mountains jutting sharp against the wide Montana sky, waiting for me to leave first.

I swung into leather, walked the horse slow across the yard. Cal moved his head to watch me. And I wondered again if I could shoot him, should it ever come to that—kill him, even in self-defense. Maybe, maybe not. You never know what you're capable of doing until the time comes for you to make a choice.

I wondered, too, if his ma had ever told Lyle about her and me. How I'd turned away from her in her time of need, because I was still wild and wanted no part of marriage and a family just then. How *her* choice, the only reasonable one open to her, had been to cast aside her pride and go straight to another man who did want to marry her. Not that it made a difference if she had told Lyle, for neither of them had ever told the boy. Nor would I, no matter what might happen between Cal and me. He had enough hate running through him as it was.

"I ain't my pa's son," the boy had said. But God help him, he was. In every way that counted he was just like his pa.

If a man doesn't fight for what belongs to him, he loses it. And once it's gone, he'll never get it back through all the long, empty years. It's gone for good. . . .

19

Lady One-Eye

Behind the long, brass-trimmed bar in McFinn's Palace Saloon and Gaming Parlor, Quincannon drew two more draughts from the large keg, sliced off the heads with the wooden paddle, and slid the glasses down the bar's polished surface. The Irish hard-rock miner who caught them flipped him a two-bit piece in return. "Keep the nickel change for yourself, laddie," he said.

Quincannon scowled as he rang up the twenty-cent sale. A whole nickel for himself, finally, after six hours of hard work. He debated leaving it in the register, but his Scot's blood got the best of that; he pocketed the five-cent coin. The lot of a bartender was neither an easy nor a profitable one, a fact he hadn't fully realized until the past two days. Nor was it a proper undertaking for a man who no longer drank strong waters of any kind. He cursed himself for a rattle-pate. Adopting the guise of a mixologist had been his blasted idea, not Amos McFinn's.

For the moment there were no more customers at his station. Most of the miners and sports lining the mahogany were watching the square, raised platform in the center of the cavernous room, where the two women faced each other across a green baize, green-skirted poker table. The play between the pair had been going on for nearly three hours now. At first the other gaming tables—poker, faro, roulette, chuck-a-luck, vingt-et-un—had had their usual heavy clutch of players. But the spectacle of the two lady gamblers engaged in a moderately high-stakes stud poker challenge was too enticing. The number of kibitzers around the platform, watching the flash of cards reflected in the huge overhead mirrors, doubled when it became apparent that Lady One-Eye's opponent, the Saint Louis Rose, was a formidable mechanic in her own right. Now the crowd had swelled so large that some of the nearby tables had been shut down for the duration.

The fact that the two women were complete opposites added to the appeal of their match. The older by ten years, Lady One-Eye was dark-haired, dark-complected; her dress was of black velvet and encased her big-boned body so totally that only her head and her long-fingered white hands were revealed. The black velvet patch covering her blind left eye gave her a faintly sinister aspect. She sat quietly and played quietly, seldom speaking, but she was nonetheless a fierce competitor who asked no quarter and granted none. The only times her steely one-eyed gaze left the cards was when she glanced at the tall, handsome gent who sat at a nearby table—her gambler husband, John Diamond, who called himself Jack O'Diamonds.

The Saint Louis Rose cut a slimmer and far gaudier figure. Too gaudy by half, in Quincannon's judgment. She wore a fancy sateen dress of bright scarlet, fashioned low across the bosom and high at the knee so that a great deal of creamy skin was exposed. A lemon-yellow wig done in ringlets, half a pound of rouge and powder, false eyelashes the size of daddy-long-legs, and a mouth painted blood-crimson completed her outlandish image. She laughed often and too loudly and was shamelessly flirtatious with the kibitzers. Even Jack O'Diamonds now and then let his gaze stray from his wife—and from the sultry presence of Lily Dumont, at whose faro bank he sat—to rest on the Rose's swelling bosom.

Quincannon was one of the few people in the hall not paying attention to the game. As they had all evening, even while he was serving customers, his eyes roamed the packed room in search of odd or furtive behavior. No weapons were permitted inside the Palace, but none of the patrons would have stood still for enforced searches by McFinn's bouncers. Quincannon was willing to wager that there were a score of hide-out guns in the hall on any given night.

Movement to his left caught the edge of his vision and turned his head. But it was only Amos McFinn once more slipping around behind the plank. He was a nervous little gent, McFinn, even at the best of times; on this night he hopped and twitched like a man doused with itching powder. Sweat gleamed on his bald dome. The ends of his mustache curled around his down-turned mouth as if they were pincers.

He drew Quincannon to the back-bar and asked in a hoarse whisper: "Anything suspicious?" It was the fifth or sixth time he'd come to voice the question. He had spent most of the evening shuttling back and forth among the half dozen bouncers spotted around the hall and Quincannon behind the bar.

"Only two small things, Mister McFinn. Your actions being one of them."

"Eh? *My* actions?"

"Stopping by to chat every half hour or so. Someone might wonder why the owner of this establishment is so interested in his new mixologist."

"No one is paying any attention to us."

"Not at the moment. At least not overtly."

"Well, I can't help worrying that he's here tonight," McFinn said. "Not that I expect he'll make an attempt in front of so many witnesses, and yet. . . ."

Quincannon was silent, his gaze roaming again. McFinn knew as well as he did that a packed room was an ideal place for an attempted murder. Especially if the person was de-ranged enough not to have much fear for his own safety.

McFinn sighed and said: "All right, I'll leave you be." He started to do this and then stopped and leaned close again. "Two small things, you said. What's the other?"

"Jack O'Diamonds."

"Eh?"

"Have you noticed his interest in Lily Dumont?"

"No. Lily Dumont?"

"They've been thick at her table for more than an hour."

"You mean you think they . . . ?"

"More than likely, yes."

"I don't believe it. Why, Jack is devoted to Lady One-Eye. I'd stake my life on it."

Then your life, Quincannon thought wryly, *is worth less than a plugged nickel.*

One of the reasons he'd chosen the guise of a bartender was that gaming hall employees were far more likely to pass along private knowledge to a fellow drone than to a detective or even a customer. A bouncer and one of the other bartenders had both confided that Lily and Jack O'Diamonds had spent time alone at her cottage on more than one occasion. They had also told him Lily's swain, a Nevada City saloon owner named Glen Bonnifield, knew about the affair and was in a rage over it. Quincannon had had proof of this. Bonnifield, a tall thin gent in a flowered vest, was in the crowd tonight, and the look in his eye as he watched Lily and Jack O'Diamonds was little short of murderous.

Lily seemed not to care that she was being observed by either Bonnifield or Lady One-Eye. Several times she had pressed close to Diamond and whispered in his ear, and she did so again now. From the look on the gambler's face, she had passed a comment of a highly intimate nature. He nodded and smiled at her—a rather lusty smile—and touched the three-carat diamond stickpin in his cravat, his trademark

23

and good-luck charm. His wife's single eye was on her cards; she didn't seem to notice. But Bonnifield did, and his smoldering look kindled and flared. He took a step toward them, changed his mind, and held his ground.

McFinn was saying: "Even if there is something between Jack and Lily, what does it have to do with the reasons . . . either of the reasons . . . I hired you?" He paused, and then blinked. "Unless you think one of them . . . ?"

"I don't think anything at this point," Quincannon said.

This was an evasion, but McFinn accepted it and let the matter drop. As he twitched away, a ripple passed through the crowd. Lady One-Eye had won another hand, this time with a spade flush over the Saint Louis Rose's high two pair. Someone at the bar said that it was the fifth pot in a row she'd taken. Quincannon glanced up at the ceiling mirrors. Early on, the pile of red and blue chips had been tall in front of the Rose; in the past hour it had begun to dwindle there, to grow on Lady One-Eye's side. One or two more large pots and she would have picked the Rose clean.

Lady One-Eye shuffled the cards for another deal, her long fingers manipulating them with practiced skill. According to the story she'd told McFinn, a buggy accident eight years ago had claimed her left eye and damaged her left hip so that she was unable to walk without the aid of her gold-knobbed cane. But she considered herself fortunate because her hands were her livelihood and both had come through the accident unscathed. Her handicap, in fact, had won her sympathy and support among the sports who frequented gaming halls such as the Palace. Even hard-bitten professional gamblers, who considered it bad luck to play against a one-eyed man, had been known to sit at a poker table with Lady One-Eye. Only once, though, in most cases, since their luck with a one-eyed woman generally turned out to be just as bad.

Five-card stud was her game, the only game she would permit at her table. And the table here *was* hers; she rented it from McFinn, paying a premium because alone on the raised platform it was the Palace's central attraction. She had occupied it for eight weeks now, ever since she and Jack O'Diamonds had arrived in Grass Valley from Tombstone, by way of Sacramento. Already word of her skill and phenomenal luck had spread wide. She never refused a game, even for low stakes, and so far she had not lost a single high-stakes match, once taking $8,000 from a Rough and Ready placer miner and on another occasion relieving a Sacramento brewer of $2,000 on a single hand of stud. Some said she was a better mechanic than such sporting queens as Poker Alice, Madame Mustache, Lurline Monte Verde, and Kitty the Schemer. A few claimed she was the equal of King Fisher, Luke Short, even Dick Clark.

At least one thought she might be a cheat to rival George Devol, the legendary Mississippi River skin-game artist. That lone skeptic was not a victim of her talents, fair or foul. He was the one person, other than the Lady and her husband, who had benefited most from her presence in the Palace: Amos McFinn.

McFinn ran a clean establishment. He had to in order to remain in business. Grass Valley—and its close neighbor, Nevada City—were no longer the wide-open, hell-roaring mining camps they'd once been. Now, five years from the new century, they were settled communities with schools, churches, and Civic Betterment Leagues. There was a move afoot to ban gambling in both towns. So far McFinn and the other gaming parlor operators had managed to forestall the efforts of the bluenoses, but if it came out that a female tinhorn had been working the Palace with impunity for eight weeks, it might just give the anti-gambling faction enough ammunition to shut down McFinn and the others along with him.

This was one reason why McFinn had hired Carpenter and Quincannon, Professional Detective Services. Lady One-Eye had increased the number of his customers and thereby his profits; he couldn't afford to send her packing on a fearful hunch, without proof. He had to know, one way or another, before he could act—and as quickly as possible.

The other reason he'd sought the help of detectives was just as urgent and potentially even more disastrous. Four days ago an anonymous note written in green ink had been slipped under the door of the room Lady One-Eye shared with Jack O'Diamonds in the Holbrooke Hotel. She'd found it and taken it to McFinn, who in turn had brought it to Sheriff Jeremiah Thorpe. But there was little the law could do. The note might well have been the work of a crackpot, all blather and bunkum. On the other hand, it might be just what it seemed: a thinly veiled death threat. Quincannon had examined the note in Thorpe's office shortly after the Nevada County Narrow Gage Railway deposited him in Grass Valley. It read:

WARNING
TO LADY ONE-EYE AND J. DIAMOND

The good citizens of Grass Valley don't want your kind. We have got rid of bunko steerers, confidence sharks, sure thing men, thimble riggers and monte throwers, and we will get rid of women card sharps and there men, too. Leave town in 48 hours or you will pay the price and pay dear when you least expect it. I mean what I say. I have fixed your kind before, permanent.

Crude language and spelling, and poor penmanship as well. It might have been written by a near illiterate with a misguided moral streak; this was McFinn's assessment. But Quincannon wondered. It could also have been written by someone educated and clever, with a motive for wanting the pair dead that had little or nothing to do with their professions. In any case, they had ignored the warning and the forty-eight hour period had passed. If the note writer carried out his threat, particularly if he carried it out inside the Palace, McFinn would be ruined as effectively as if Lady One-Eye were exposed as a cheat. . . .

"Three fives! The pot's mine, dearie!"

The Saint Louis Rose's loud, coarse voice echoed through the hall. Quincannon frowned and glanced up at the mirror above the poker table; the Rose was dragging in a small pile of red and blue chips. Lady One-Eye watched her stoically.

"Two in a row now and more to come," the Rose said to a knot of bearded miners close on her left. "My luck is changing for fair, gents. It won't be long before all the red and blue pretties are mine to fondle."

The knot of miners sent up a small cheer of encouragement. Most of the onlookers, however, remained Lady One-Eye's champions. Like them, Quincannon wished the Rose would close her mouth and play her game in silence. Listening to her plume herself was an irritation and a distraction.

The deal was Lady One-Eye's. Without speaking she picked up the deck. Again, Quincannon studied her dexterous fingers as they manipulated the deck, set it out to be cut, then dealt one card face down and one face up to the Rose and herself. If she was a skin-game artist, he reflected, she was in a class by herself.

The professionals she'd cleaned over the past eight weeks would have caught her out if she had been doing anything as obvious as dealing seconds, dealing off the bottom, switching hole cards, or using a mirror or other reflective surface to reveal the faces of the cards to her as she dealt them. She wasn't using advantage cards: the house provided sealed decks, which were opened in plain view at the table, and switching them for marked decks hidden in her clothing was next to impossible for a woman who wore a high-collared dress with long, tight-fitting sleeves. Nor could her gaff be table bags or any of the other fancy contraptions manufactured by the likes of Will & Fink, the notorious San Francisco firm that specialized in supplying gimmicks to crooked gamblers. Because of the raised platform, and the fact that a woman played upon it, the table wore its floor-length green skirt, but the skirt was drawn up until Lady One-Eye took her chair, thus allowing potential players to examine both it and the table if they chose to. Table tricks were the cheap grifter's ploy anyway. And Lady One-Eye was anything but a cheap grifter.

The Rose's up card was the jack of clubs, the Lady's the four of hearts. Both women checked their hole cards, then the Rose winked at her admirers, bet twenty dollars. Lady One-Eye called and dealt a ten of diamonds to go with the jack, a deuce of spades for herself. This time the Rose bet fifty dollars. Again, silently, Lady One-Eye called.

The fourth round of cards brought the Rose a spade jack, the Lady a five of diamonds. The challenger grinned at her high pair and said—"Jacks have never let me down."—a remark that caused Lady One-Eye to cast an almost imperceptible sidelong glance at her husband. "One hundred dollars on the pair of 'em, dearie."

Quincannon wondered if the remark was deliberate—if the Rose, too, had noticed the intimacy between Jack O'Diamonds and Lily Dumont. Lady One-Eye was aware of it, of that he was fairly certain.

Without another glance at her hole card, the Lady called.

Slowly she dealt the fifth and final cards. Jack of hearts. And for herself, the three of clubs.

The onlookers began to stir and murmur. Play at the few other open tables suspended for the moment. Everyone in the Palace stood or sat watching the two women. Even McFinn, leaning against one of the roulette lay-outs, was motionless for the time being.

"Well, dearie," the Rose said, "three pretty little jacks to your possible straight." She tapped her hole card. "Is this the fourth jack I have here? It may well be. What do you think, Lady, of my having the jack of diamonds?"

To Quincannon, the innuendo was plain. But whatever Lady One-Eye thought of it, she neither reacted nor responded.

"Or it may be another ten. A full house beats a straight all to hell, dearie. If you've even got a six or an ace to fill."

"Bet your jacks," Lady One-Eye said coldly.

The Rose's sly smile faded. She separated four blue chips from her small remaining stack, slid them into the pot. "Two hundred dollars says you don't have a six or an ace, and it doesn't matter if you do."

"Your two hundred and raise another two."

Voices created an excited buzzing, ebbed again to total silence. Neither of the women seemed to notice. Their gazes were not fixed on each other.

"A bluff, dearie?" the Rose said.

"Call or raise and you'll soon know."

"Four hundred is all I have left."

"Call or raise."

"Your two hundred, then, and raise my last two hundred."

"Call."

The pile of red and blue chips bulged between them. The crowd was expectantly still as the Rose shrugged and turned over her hole card.

The queen of hearts. No help.

"Three jacks," she said. "Beat 'em if you can."

Her one good eye as icy as any Quincannon had ever seen, Lady One-Eye flipped her hole card. And when it was revealed in the glistening mirrors, a triumphant shout went up from her admirers.

Ace of clubs to fill the straight.

The pot and all of the Rose's table stakes were hers.

For the next half hour Quincannon was busy attending to the reborn thirst of the customers. But not so busy that he was unable to maintain his observations.

The Saint Louis Rose, after fending off a pair of drunken sports who considered her fair game, slipped quietly out of the hall. Lady One-Eye gathered her winnings and cashed them in, all the while keeping watch on her husband and Lily Dumont. Jack O'Diamonds didn't stay long at Lily's faro bank, nor did he approach his wife. Instead, he stepped up to the bar and called for forty-rod whisky. The Nevada City saloonkeeper, Glen Bonnifield, took this opportunity to stalk to Lily's table, lean down with his face close to hers. Their conversation was brief and heated. Then Bonnifield slapped the table hard with his open hand—as a substitute for slapping Lily, Quincannon thought—and swung away, back past the bar. His gaze met Diamond's in the mirror, the two struck sparks, but neither man made a move toward the other. Bonnifield stalked to the front entrance and was gone.

Quincannon served Jack O'Diamonds his whisky. "Your wife had a fine run of luck tonight, Mister Diamond."

"My wife's luck is always fine." The gambler didn't sound pleased about it. Jealousy? Compared to Lady One-Eye's skill with the pasteboards, honest or not, his own was mediocre.

"And your luck with Lily? Has that been fine, too?"

The comment produced a tight-lipped glower. "What do you mean by that?"

"No offense, sir," Quincannon blandly. "Mister Bonnifield seemed to think it was, that's all."

"I don't give a damn what Bonnifield thinks," Jack O'Diamonds said. He fingered his flashy diamond stickpin, downed his whisky at a gulp. Then he, too, left the Palace—alone, and still without speaking to his wife.

Lady One-Eye took her leave five minutes later, in the company of the two burly bouncers assigned by McFinn as escorts. But first she approached Lily Dumont and engaged her in a brief, heated discussion, just as Bonnifield had. Lily's reaction to whatever was said to her was to call the Lady an unlady-like name in a voice loud enough to turn heads. Lady One-Eye responded by making a warning gesture with her gold-knobbed cane.

Quincannon decided he'd had enough of bartending, for tonight if not for the rest of his life. He hung up his apron, donned his coat and derby hat, helped himself to half a dozen cheroots from a cigar vase on the bar, and went to pay Lily a visit himself.

She was shuffling and cutting a full deck of cards for placement in her tiger-decorated faro box; the cards made angry, snapping sounds in her slim fingers. She, too, was a complete opposite of Lady One-Eye. She had flaming red hair, a volatile temper to match, and the hot sparking eyes of a Gypsy. Fire to the Lady's ice.

"Trouble with Her Majesty?" Quincannon asked sympathetically.

"Her Majesty. Hah. I'll tell you what that female is." Which Lily proceeded to do in language that would have made a hard-rock miner blink.

"A cold and jealous one, all right," he agreed.

31

"Threaten me, will she? I'll fix her first. I'll rip out her other eye and turn her into Lady Blind."

"Why did she threaten you?"

"Never mind about that."

Quincannon shrugged. "What does Jack O'Diamonds see in her?"

"Money, of course. But maybe not for much longer."

"Oh? He wouldn't be planning to leave her, would he?"

"That's none of your business."

"Is it any of yours, Lily?"

"Miss Dumont to you. My business is mine, no one else's."

"Not even Glen Bonnifield's?"

"Damn Glen Bonnifield. Damn Lady One-Eye. And damn *you*."

As Quincannon made his way toward the front entrance, he spied Amos McFinn moving hurriedly through the crowd to intercept him. He pretended not to see the Palace's owner; he had no interest in answering the "Anything suspicious?" question yet again. He managed to make good his escape before McFinn got close enough to ask it.

It was some past midnight now, and the mountain air was chill. Even though June was not far off, snow still mantled the Sierras' higher elevations. Grass Valley's hilly streets were deserted; the only sounds were the faint throb of a piano in one of the nearby saloons, the continual beat of the stamps at the big Empire Mine southeast of town. A far cry from the boom years of Grass Valley and Nevada City, following the 1851 discovery of gold in quartz ledges buried beneath the earth, when thousands of gold-seekers, camp followers, and Cornish and Irish hard-rock miners had clogged the streets day and night. Even on Quincannon's first visit here, more than a dozen years ago, the town had still retained some of its

Gold Rush flavor. Now nearly all the rough edges had been buffed down and rounded off. This was fine if you were a law-abiding, church-going citizen with children to raise. But tame places were not for John Quincannon. He would rather walk the streets of a hell-roaring gold camp, or even those of the Barbary Coast.

He paused on the boardwalk to light one of the cheroots he had appropriated. He preferred a pipe to cigars, but free to-bacco had a greater satisfaction than the paid-for kind. Then, instead of turning upstreet to the Holbrooke Hotel, where he had engaged a room, he walked downhill to the town's main thoroughfare, Mill Street. The only lighted building along there was the Empire Livery Stable. He saw the night hostler working inside as he passed—and no one else before or after he turned uphill on Neal Street.

The bouncer at McFinn's had told him that Lily Dumont's cottage was on Pleasant Street, just off Neal. He found it with no difficulty—a tiny frame building, of no more than three rooms, tucked well back from the street in the shade of a pair of live oaks. The neighborhood was a good one, and by the starlight he could tell that the cottage and its gardens were well set up. Much too well set up, he thought, for a woman who operated a faro bank to afford on her own. He wondered if Glen Bonnifield had an investment in the property.

The cottage's curtained windows were dark; so were those in the two nearest houses. He shed the remains of his cheroot and walked softly around to the rear. The back door was not locked. He entered, struck a lucifer to orient himself and to show him the way into the front parlor.

An oil lamp with a red silk shade sat atop a writing desk. He lit the wick, turning the flame low, and by this light he searched the desk. There was one bottle of ink, but it was blue, not green. Nothing else in the desk held any interest for him. He carried the lamp into Lily's bedroom, where he found further evidence of financial aid: satin dresses, a white fox capote, an expensive ostrich-feather hat. But that was all he found. If Lily had written the threatening note, she had either done it elsewhere or gotten rid of the bottle of ink she'd used.

Quincannon returned the lamp to the writing desk, snuffed the wick, then followed the flicker of another match to the rear door. He let himself out, shut the door quietly behind him.

He was just turning onto the path toward the front when the first bullet sang close past his right ear.

He went down instantly, a reflex action that saved his life: the second bullet slashed air where his head had been. The booming echo of the shots filled his ears. He reached under his coat for his Navy Colt, then remembered that he hadn't worn it because of his bartending duties; instead, he'd armed himself with a double-barreled Remington Derringer, an effective weapon at close quarters in a crowded room but with a range of no more than twenty feet. He rolled sideways, clawing the Derringer free of his pocket, half expecting to feel the shock of another bullet. But there were no more shots. The thorny wood of a rose bush ended his roll; grimacing, he shoved away, and then lay flat and still, the Derringer up in front of him. He peered through the darkness, listening.

Running footsteps. Fading, then gone.

He pushed onto his knees. Lamplight suddenly brightened one of the windows in the house next door; its out-spill showed him that the yard and the street in front were now deserted. He got quickly to his feet, careful to keep his head turned aside from the light. A face peered out through the lamp-lit window and a voice hollered: "What in tarnation's going on out there?" Quincannon didn't answer. Staying in the shadows, he ran ahead and looked both ways along Pleasant Street.

His assailant had vanished.

"Hell and damn!" he muttered angrily under his breath. He slid the Derringer back into his pocket, and hurried to Neal and around the corner before any of Lily's neighbors came out to investigate.

Grass Valley a tame place now, its streets safe at night? Bah! There was still plenty of hell left in this camp. The question was, was it hell directed at him or someone else?

The Holbrooke, a two-story brick edifice on East Main, was Grass Valley's oldest and finest hostelry. Presidents Grant, Harrison, Cleveland, and Garfield had stayed there during visits to California, so had Gentleman Jim Corbett. And so had the notorious gold country highwayman, Black Bart—a fact the management chose not to advertise. If any of the hotel's distinguished guests had ever wandered uphill in Texas Tommy's Golden Gate Brothel, a nearby attraction in the old days, this fact was also held in discreet confidence.

The gas-lit lobby was deserted when Quincannon entered. Gaslight flickered even more dimly in the upstairs hallways; electricity had yet to be installed here. He made his way, first, to the door of Number 3, the room occupied by Lady One-Eye and Jack O'Diamonds. No light showed around its edges, and, when he pressed his ear to the panel, he heard nothing from within. From there he went around past Number 8, his room, and stopped before Number 11 at the rear. It was no more than five seconds before the latch clicked and the door opened.

He said: "The Saint Louis Rose, I presume?"

"Hello, dearie." She caught hold of his coat sleeve, tugged

35

him inside, and quickly shut the door. "You're late. I expected you an hour ago."

"I've been to Lily Dumont's cottage."

"Have you now. For what purpose?"

"Not the one you're thinking. She has too many admirers already."

"John Diamond, for one."

"So you noticed that, too. I thought you had."

"Lady One-Eye is also aware of it."

He nodded. "Trouble there, do you think?"

"Of one kind or another. Lily Dumont is a dish to tempt any man, especially one with a block of ice for a wife."

"I prefer loud and bawdy blondes myself." Quincannon gave her a broad wink. "Come over here, Rosie, and give me a kiss."

"I will not. Stand your distance."

"The Saint Louis Rose is no more likely than Lily Dumont to refuse a handsome man a kiss. Or anything else he might want."

"Perhaps not. But Sabina Carpenter is and you know it."

"To my great sorrow."

Quincannon sighed and went to sit on one of the room's plush chairs. He gazed wistfully at his partner in Carpenter and Quincannon, Professional Detective Services, and the object of his unrequited affection. She had removed all of the bawd's rouge and powder and false eyelashes, and shed the ridiculous ringlet wig. The transformation was amazing. In place of the hard, vulgar, blonde Rose was a mature, well-bred, dark-haired woman with more than a dozen years of experience as a detective, six of those with the Pinkerton Agency's Denver office.

"What did you mean by loud and bawdy?" she demanded. "Do you think I overplayed my rôle tonight?"

"Perhaps a touch," he said tactfully.

"I thought my performance was rather good."

"It's too bad Lotta Crabtree wasn't here to see it. She might have offered you a new career as a stage actress."

"Don't make fun of me, John. I didn't strike a false note with Lady One-Eye, I'm certain of that."

"She was too busy plucking you like a chicken," Quincannon said. "How much did you lose, by the way? The entire fifteen hundred McFinn gave you?"

"Yes. Mostly on that last hand."

"A straight to your three jacks. Luck of the cards, or did she manufacture her own luck?"

"Oh, she's a skin-game artist, all right," Sabina said. "One of the best I've seen."

"Were you able to spot her gaff?"

"I think so. But she's so good at it that it took me most of the night. I wouldn't have seen it at all if I hadn't spent those weeks with Jim Moon at the Oyster Ocean in Denver a few years ago, learning his bag of tricks. It boils down to manipulating the cards so she knows her opponent's hole card on every hand she deals."

In gathering the cards for her deal, Sabina explained, Lady One-Eye dropped her own last hand on top of the deck, the five cards having been arranged so that the lowest was on top and the highest was second in line. As she did this, she gave the five cards a quick squeeze, which produced a slight convex longitudinal bend. During the shuffle, she maneuvered the five-card slug to the top of the deck. Then, just before offering the deck for the cut, she buried the slug in the middle, at the point where her opponent tended to cut each time. The crimp in the cards ensured that the slug would be returned to the top. All she had to do then was to deal fairly, flexing the deck once or twice first to take out the slug's bend.

The first card she dealt, which she knew from memory, was therefore the opponent's hole card. And her hole card, the second in line, was always higher.

"Clever," Quincannon said. "The advantage is small, but for a sharp it's enough to control almost any game."

Sabina nodded. "But I'd like to play her once more . . . or rather, Rose would . . . to make absolutely sure I'm right about her gaff. An hour or so should do it. Will McFinn stake me to another five hundred, do you suppose?"

"Probably, but we needn't stretch his patience. I'll stake you, my dear. If you lose, we'll add the sum to McFinn's bill."

"He might refuse to pay the extra charge."

"No matter. I'll accept your favors as reimbursement."

His boldness, as always, exasperated her. "You never give up, do you, John?"

"Never. You may as well say yes now and enjoy the consequences. I'll wear down your resistance sooner or later."

"No, you won't. The answer is no, and it always will be no. Why can't you accept that we're business partners, nothing more?"

Quincannon sighed again, elaborately this time. But he wasn't daunted. He could be a very patient man when the situation warranted. He consoled himself with this, and with the pious thought that his intentions, after all, were honorable. Simple seduction had long ago ceased to be his primary motivation.

"To get back to business," Sabina said, "I don't intend to lose to Lady One-Eye tomorrow night. I know ways to counteract her gaff, thanks to Jim Moon."

"Either way, we'll have to put an end to the matter then. The sooner McFinn sends the Lady packing, the better off he'll be. It seems likely now that the threatening note is genuine."

"Now? Has something happened?"

"At Lily Dumont's cottage. Two rounds from a heavy revolver nearly took my head off."

"John! Someone tried to kill you? Who?"

"I didn't get a look at him. Too dark."

"Was there any light where you were?"

"No."

"Then whoever it was couldn't see you clearly, either."

"Only my shape as I left the cottage. If you're thinking he might have mistaken me for someone else, you're right . . . he might well have."

"Jack O'Diamonds?"

"Or Glen Bonnifield. If it wasn't Bonnifield who did the shooting."

"Isn't he Lily Dumont's lover?"

"Evidently."

"Is he the reason you went to her cottage?"

"One of them," Quincannon said. "Lily's involvement with Jack O'Diamonds seems more than a simple dalliance. It occurred to me that she might have written the note, either in a foolish effort to drive Lady One-Eye out of town or as a clever ploy to pave the way for an attempt on the Lady's life."

"Did you find evidence to incriminate her?"

"None. No bottle of green ink."

Sabina nodded thoughtfully. "If Bonnifield is the jealous sort, *he* could be the author of the note."

"That he could. He was at the Palace tonight, glaring daggers at both Lily and Jack."

"Well. This business seems to be more complicated than we first believed."

"And more dangerous," Quincannon said. "Be on your guard tomorrow, Sabina. Take that little one-shot Derringer of yours along to the Palace, just in case."

"It's already in my bag." She smiled impishly at him. "And knowing that, aren't you glad you didn't try to do more than just talk me into bed just now?"

In the morning Quincannon hired a horse at the Empire Livery and rode the three miles to Nevada City. He spent the better part of four hours making the rounds of saloons—one of them Glen Bonnifield's Ace High—and local merchant establishments, pretending to be a patent medicine drummer and asking sly questions. He learned several things about Bonnifield and the saloonkeeper's relationship with Lily Dumont, a few of potential significance.

Bonnifield was, in fact, keeping Lily in her Grass Valley cottage and had been for two years. He was as hot-tempered as she and jealous to a fault; a year ago he had threatened to shoot a man who had been pestering her. And he carried a Buntline Special Colt with a twelve-inch barrel, a weapon with which he was reported to be an excellent shot.

A dangerous man, Bonnifield. But one of direct action, not devious design. Would such a man be likely to write a note forewarning both a rival and the rival's wife? Quincannon was left with the impression that the answer was a definite no.

When he returned to Grass Valley, he went first to the Holbrooke. There was no message from Sabina at the desk, as there would have been if she'd learned anything important she felt he should know. Then he walked downstreet to the Palace.

By day, in the harsh glare of the sun, the gambling hall had an uninviting look. Like nearly all of the commercial buildings in Grass Valley, it was made of brick—the consequence of a disastrous fire in 1855 that had consumed the township's three hundred wooden structures, leaving nothing standing but Wells Fargo's brick and iron vault and a dozen scorched brick chimneys. The massive sign above the door had a warped and faded look. The brass fittings of the red-globed gaslights were pitted with rust. Little wonder, Quincannon thought, that the bluenoses were bent on closing it and its sisters down. Some of the other gambling parlors here and in Nevada City had even tawdrier daylight appearances.

The Saint Louis Rose was not inside, nor was Lady One-Eye, Jack O'Diamonds, or Lily Dumont. McFinn was, however. He spied Quincannon, hurried up, and plucked nervously at his sleeve.

"Well? Have you found out anything?"

"Nothing to be confided just yet, Mister McFinn."

"That's just what your lady friend. . . ."

"The Saint Louis Rose, you mean."

"Yes, yes, the Saint Louis Rose. That's just what she said when I spoke to her earlier. When will the two of you have something to confide? Eh?"

"Tonight, perhaps."

"When tonight?"

"After the Rose and Lady One-Eye have another game."

"Another game," McFinn said. "And another five hundred dollars of my money in the Lady's purse, I suppose."

"The Rose asked you for an additional stake, did she?"

"Yes, and I let her talk me into giving it to her."

"Pity. I was hoping she'd come to me instead."

"Are you sure she knows the game of poker?"

"Better than you or I, and as well as Lady One-Eye," Quincannon assured him. "Don't worry. Your money is being well spent."

"I'll consider it well spent if nothing calamitous happens," McFinn said mournfully. "I can't help feeling that disaster lurks close by."

"You're wrong, sir. It doesn't."

41

The one who was wrong, however, was John Quincannon.

At five o'clock, in fresh clothing and with a plate of liver and onions residing comfortably under his vest, Quincannon returned to the Palace to resume his duties behind the bar. Lily Dumont appeared shortly afterward and began setting up her faro bank. She spoke to no one. She seemed preoccupied tonight—and almost as nervous as McFinn. Quincannon wondered if the cause of her agitation was that she'd gotten wind of the shooting last night.

Lady One-Eye and Jack O'Diamonds arrived together, but they soon parted without a word to each other. The Lady took her place at the platform table and was immediately challenged by a pair of whiskered gents who had the look of *nouveau riche* prospectors. Diamond made his way to the bar, where he drank two whiskies in short order. Then he moved restlessly about the room, stopping for a while to play vingt-et-un, and then again to play faro. But it was not Lily's bank that he chose. He avoided going anywhere near her, as if she were not even on the premises. Lily, likewise, paid not the slightest attention to him. A falling-out between them? Or was there another reason for their ignoring of each other?

The next to arrive was the Saint Louis Rose, wearing a purple dress that was even more revealing than last night's scarlet number. *Where did she get such outfits?* Quincannon wondered. *Rent them or buy them?* For all he knew, Sabina had a closet full of such costumes and led a wanton double life, slipping out once or twice a week to Barbary Coast deadfalls. It made him feel testy to see the men in the hall ogling her bared flesh. As if he were a jealous husband. Which—and he might as well admit it—was what he wished he was.

The Rose joined Jack O'Diamonds at the faro table and attempted to engage him in conversation. He spurned her; he seemed as preoccupied as Lily Dumont. Three times in less than an hour he ordered whisky from one of the percentage girls. But it seemed to have little or no effect on him.

Lady One-Eye made short work of the two prospectors, taking several hundred dollars from one and nearly a thousand from the other. They accepted their losses good-naturedly, offering to buy her a magnum of champagne as a token of their esteem for her skills. She declined. There was a tight set to her mouth tonight, a distracted, mechanical quality to her movements. Trouble with her husband over Lily Dumont?

Shortly after the prospectors left her alone on the platform, Glen Bonnifield walked in. Or, more precisely, weaved in. His face was dark-flushed, his eyes bloodshot, his expression brooding: the look of a man who had spent a good part of the day in close company with a bottle of forty-rod, and not for pleasurable reasons. He lurched up to Quincannon's station, stood for a few seconds glowering in the direction of Lily Dumont. Then he called for whisky.

Quincannon said politely: "Carrying a bit of a load tonight, eh, Mister Bonnifield?"

"What if I am? No concern of yours."

"No, sir, except that you forgot to check your weapon."

"My what?"

"The Buntline Special poking out from under your coat."

"No damn' concern of yours," Bonnifield growled. He spat into one of the knee-high cuspidors. "Pour my whisky, barman, and be quick about it."

"Not until you check your weapon."

"Well, now. Why don't you try checking it for me?"

His voice was loud, belligerent; some of the other patrons swung their heads to stare at him. So did Lily Dumont. When she saw the condition he was in, her nervousness evolved into visible fright.

"Let's not have any trouble, Mister Bonnifield."

"There'll be plenty of trouble tonight, by God."

Abruptly Bonnifield shoved away from the rail, staggered over to Lily's faro bank. She shrank back while two of her customers scurried out of harm's way. Quincannon was on the run through the notch in the bar by then. He heard McFinn shout a warning to his bouncers; he also glimpsed Jack O'Diamonds jump up and start past the platform to Lily's defense.

What remained of Bonnifield's self-control had dissolved in drunken fury. He yelled—"You little tramp, I won't let you make a fool out of me!"—and his hand groped under his coat for the Buntline Special.

Quincannon reached for the saloonkeeper just as he drew the big-barreled gun, knocked his arm down before he could trigger a shot. Bonnifield swung wildly with his other hand, struck Quincannon's shoulder a glancing blow that drove him backward. Two of the bouncers muscled up; they caught hold of Bonnifield, tried to wrestle him into submission. He broke free and stumbled into a confused grouping of customers and Palace employees, still clutching his Buntline Special. Men shouted; a woman let out a shrill cry of alarm.

In the midst of all this ferment, a single shot sounded, low and popping, like the explosion of a Fourth of July firecracker. A man grunted loudly in pain. That and the shot ended the budding mêlée, parted the crowd in a fashion that was almost Biblical. Quincannon saw a number of things in that instant. He saw the two bouncers drive Bonnifield to the floor and disarm him. He saw Lily rush out from behind her faro table. He saw Sabina running toward him. He saw Lady One-Eye seated at her table, one hand on the green baize and the other at the bodice of her dress. And in the cleared space where the mass of people had fallen back on both sides, he saw the victim of the gunshot lying supine and motionless, blood staining the right side of his coat at heart level.

Lily shrieked: "It's Jack! Oh no, it's *Jack!*"

She flung herself to the carpet beside Jack O'Diamonds, laid her flaming red head against his chest. When she lifted it again, her eyes were wet with tears: "He's not breathing . . . he's dead."

Some of the men closed in and helped her to her feet. Immediately she shook a clenched fist at Glen Bonnifield, who was kneeling a few feet away. "You did it! Damn you, Glen, *you* killed him!"

Bonnifield was dazed from his scuffle with the bouncers; if he heard her, he made no reply. One of the bouncers held the Buntline Special. Quincannon stepped over to him, took the weapon, and felt and then sniffed the barrel. "Not with this, he didn't. It hasn't been fired."

McFinn came dancing up, his eyes as wide as a toad's. "Then who did shoot him? Quincannon, you blasted sorry excuse for a fly cop, did you see who pulled the trigger?"

Quincannon admitted that he hadn't. He glanced at Sabina; her face told him she hadn't, either.

"Did anyone see who fired that shot?" the little man roared over the babble of voices.

No one had. Or, at least, no one who would own up to being a witness.

Beside himself now, McFinn bellowed to his bouncers to seal off the front and rear entrances, keep everybody inside the hall. No sooner had they rushed to obey him than a new impassioned voice was raised above the others. This one belonged to Lady One-Eye, who had come down off the platform and was standing stock-still next to the remains of Jack O'Diamonds, pointing with her cane.

"Look at that!" she cried, her good eye blazing with cold

fire. "Some blackguard not only murdered my husband in cold blood, he stole Jack's diamond stickpin, too!"

She sounded more upset over the loss of his stickpin than she did over the loss of his life.

Sheriff Jeremiah Thorpe was a man in his early thirties, with muttonchop whiskers and an efficient, no-nonsense manner. He took charge as soon as he and two of his deputies arrived with the bartender McFinn had dispatched to bring them. The answers to a few terse questions allowed him to separate the principal players in the drama from the extras and onlookers. These, with one exception, he herded into McFinn's private quarters at the rear, while his deputies remained in the main hall to question the others. The exception was Glen Bonnifield. One of the bouncers had fetched him a crack on the head with a bung starter in order to subdue him, and Bonnifield still hadn't regained his wits. He was being administered to by a town doctor.

Suspense crackled among the small group. Lily Dumont continued to shed tears, and Lady One-Eye was once again coldly stoic, hiding her emotions behind her poker face, but it was plain that neither was happy to learn that a pair of San Francisco detectives had been operating in their midst, even though the reason had yet to be divulged. McFinn was still in a lather. He kept glaring at Quincannon with open hostility.

Both Quincannon and Sabina had met Thorpe on their arrival in Grass Valley; he'd been friendly enough then, but the friendliness was in abeyance now. There was an edge to his voice as he said: "Well, Mister Quincannon? Can you sort out what took place here tonight?"

"He couldn't sort out a handful of poker chips," McFinn said, glaring. "Neither him nor his lady partner. I hired them to keep disaster from my door, and they failed miserably. I'll be ruined. . . ."

"Amos, hold your tongue."

"I still say Glen Bonnifield shot poor Jack," Lily said. "He hated him . . . he made no bones about that. And last night . . . there were shots fired at my cottage. That must have been Glen, too, after Jack."

"Diamond was at your place last night?"

"No. I wasn't, either, when it happened. But Glen must've thought we were there together."

"Why would he fire shots at an empty cottage?"

Quincannon said carefully: "It may be that he was hiding outside and mistook a shadow for a man." Declaring that *he* had been the mistaken target would serve no purpose except to vex the sheriff. He had, after all, entered Lily's home illegally, and he had also failed to report the shooting.

Thorpe asked him: "So then you agree that Bonnifield killed Diamond?"

"No. It was Bonnifield last night but not tonight."

"How do you know it wasn't?"

"He carried a Buntline Special. I examined it before you came, and it hadn't been fired. Also, the report of a Buntline is loud, booming. The shot that folded Jack O'Diamonds was low and popping, like a firecracker."

"A small caliber weapon, then."

"Yes. A Derringer or a pocket revolver."

"Does Bonnifield carry a hide-out weapon, Miss Dumont?"

"No. I've never seen one."

"Then who did shoot Diamond?"

"And who," Lady One-Eye said, "stole his stickpin?"

Quincannon said: "Lily Dumont did that."

"Her! I should've known." The Lady jabbed menacingly

at the younger woman with her cane. "You damned murdering husband-stealer. . . ."

Lily shrank away from her. "It's a lie! I didn't kill Jack . . . I swear I didn't kill him."

"But you did steal his stickpin," Quincannon insisted. "Slipped it out of his cravat when you flung yourself down beside his body, before you announced that he was dead. You were the only person close enough to've managed it without being noticed."

Sabina said wryly: "Jack O'Diamonds's handsome face wasn't his only lure for her. Money and the promise of more to come was at least part of the reason she was going away with him."

"What's that?" Thorpe said. "She was going away with Diamond?"

"All right," Lily cried, "all right, I was. And yes, I took his stickpin . . . why shouldn't I? He was dead, and he would've wanted me to have it. He loved me, and I did love him."

Lady One-Eye uttered a coarse word well known to the breeders of cattle.

"But I *didn't* shoot him. You have to believe me. I don't own a handgun . . . I don't even know how to fire one."

The sheriff turned to Quincannon. "Is she telling the truth or not?"

This was the moment Quincannon had been avoiding. For once his deductive prowess had failed him; he had no clear-cut idea of who had fired the fatal shot. He resisted an impulse to tug at his shirt collar, which now seemed a little snug.

"Ah, perhaps she is," he hedged, "and, then again, perhaps she isn't."

"What the devil does that mean?"

"It means," McFinn said scornfully, "he doesn't know

48

either way. He doesn't have a clue to the identity of Jack's murderer."

There was a small, uncomfortable silence.

Sabina broke it by saying: "Of course he does. We both know the murderer's name and how the crime was done. Don't we, John?"

He blinked at her. Her smile was faint but reassuring. *By Godfrey*, he thought, *she does know. Dear Sabina, the love of my life, the savior of my reputation . . . she knows!*

"Well?" Thorpe demanded. "Who was it?"

"Lady One-Eye, of course."

Heads swung toward the recent widow. Lady One-Eye stood in her usual ramrod-stiff posture, one hand resting on the gold knob of her cane, her good eye impaling Sabina. The only emotion it, or her expression, betrayed was contempt.

"How dare you accuse me? I might've been shot, too, to-night, the same as my husband. Have you forgotten the note that threatened both our lives?"

"I haven't forgotten it. The fact is, you wrote that note yourself."

"*I* wrote it?"

"When we were playing stud last night," Sabina said, "I noticed a fading smudge of green on your left thumb . . . green ink, the same color as the note. Chances are you didn't bother to dispose of the bottle, and the sheriff will find it in your hotel room."

"Suppose she did write the note," Thorpe said. "What was the purpose?"

Lady One-Eye said: "Yes, Rose or whatever your name is. What possible reason could I have for threatening myself and then shooting my husband?"

"He was going to leave you, that's why!" Lily shouted. The shift of suspicion from her to Lady One-Eye had relieved her and made her bold again. "He was tired of you and your cold and stingy ways. And you knew it."

"I knew nothing of the kind."

"Yes, you did. You as much as said so last night at my table. You warned me against trying to take him away from you."

"Liar. It's your word against mine."

"Oh, you knew, Lady," Sabina said. "And you planned to kill Jack if he tried to go through with it. He must have let something slip earlier today that convinced you he was leaving soon, perhaps as soon as tonight. With Lily and no doubt with some or all of the gambling winnings you accumulated. That's why you acted when you did. As for the note, you wrote that to divert suspicion from yourself . . . to make it seem as though you were also an intended victim. I'll warrant, too, that if you'd had enough time to complete your plan, you would've hidden the weapon you used at Lily's faro table or in her cottage, to frame her as the guilty party. That way, you'd have gotten your revenge on both of them."

"Sheriff," Lady One-Eye said to Thorpe, "I won't stand for any more of these outrageous accusations. How could I possibly have shot my husband? I was sitting at my table on the platform, in plain sight of the room. My hands were in plain sight, too. If I had drawn a gun and fired it, someone would surely have seen me do it."

"That's right," McFinn said, "*I* would have. I glanced at her table just before the shot and again just afterward, and she was sitting as she said, with her hands in plain sight."

"Yes, she was," Sabina agreed. "I saw her myself. One hand on the table, the other at her bosom."

"Well, then?"

"Lady One-Eye is a mistress of sleight-of-hand. She has been cheating her opponents at poker with it . . . that's right,

Mister McFinn, she *is* a skin-game artist . . . and tonight she used the same principle to shoot Jack O'Diamonds. Only in this case the sleight-of-hand only indirectly involved her hand."

"Don't talk in riddles, Missus Carpenter. How the devil did she do it?"

Sabina said: "Remember, there was general confusion at the time . . . no one was looking closely at her. Remember, too, that the lower half of her body was mostly hidden by the skirt of her dress and the table skirt." And before Lady One-Eye could stop her, Sabina leaned down, took the hem of the woman's black velvet dress, and hoisted the skirt straight up over the knee.

Quincannon, who was seldom surprised by anything any more, gaped and said—"Hell and damn!"—in utter amazement. There were similar astonished outcries from the others.

Lady One-Eye was also Lady One-Leg.

Her left leg from the knee down and her shoe-encased left foot were made of wood. And fastened with tape to the joining of foot and leg was a pearl-handled .32 caliber revolver, a long length of twine leading from its trigger up inside the dress to its bodice.

"Apparently she lost her leg in the same buggy accident that claimed her eye," Sabina said to Quincannon later, in her room at the Holbrooke. "She had two reasons for hiding the fact, I expect. One was vanity. The other was professional fear. Most sports didn't mind too much playing a woman with one eye. It added an element of spice to their games. But a woman with one eye and one leg might well have made them uneasy. You know how superstitious gamblers are. Too many would've considered a double-handicapped lady gambler to be bad luck."

"So they would," he agreed. "Now tell me how you knew the leg was wooden?"

"I bumped her occasionally last night, while we were in the midst of our game. She wore a shoe over it, as you saw, and she drew it back quickly, but the feel of the contact was odd enough to linger in my memory."

"How did you deduce the revolver fastened to it . . . the fact she'd literally shot him with her raised leg?"

"Two things," Sabina said. "One was a glimpse of the trigger string between two dress buttons. That was just after the shooting. She hadn't quite pushed it all the way inside yet."

"It might have been a thread."

"Yes, but then I remembered a man I knew once in Denver, when I was with the Pinks. He had a wooden leg and used to keep a hide-out gun strapped to it. He fired it with a spring mechanism, but it struck me that a length of twine would do just as well."

Quincannon said admiringly: "You're a clever woman, my dear. Yes, and better than I am at the detecting game more often than I'd like to admit."

"Amos McFinn doesn't consider either of us much of a detective. And with some justification, at least from his point of view."

"Poor McFinn. But Lady One-Eye's devious actions were none that we could have foreseen or prevented."

"True. Still, I feel sorry for him. He may well be ruined by tonight's events."

Quincannon was philosophical. "Ah, well, it was only a matter of time before the bluenoses had their way. Gambling parlors such as the Palace are doomed to extinction, I fear, at least in small towns like this one."

"Perhaps, but . . . John, he'll refuse to pay the balance of our fee. You know that as well as I do. What would you say to us forfeiting it, rather than suing to collect? As a gesture of good will?"

"Forfeit the balance?" Now he was aghast. "Do you mean it?"

"Yes. From a practical standpoint it would also enhance our reputation. Results guaranteed at no risk to our clients."

"My father would have been appalled." Thomas L. Quincannon, in fact, would have had any member of his Washington detective agency horsewhipped for suggesting such a thing. "So would Allan Pinkerton."

"The new century is almost upon us, John. New business practices are necessary in a new age."

"Well, I suppose we can discuss the matter. In the morning, when we're both rested."

"Yes, in the morning." At the door she said: "Did you really mean it that I'm often better in the detecting game than you?"

"I did. Though just how often I wouldn't care to say."

"Quite an admission for the likes of you." She favored him with a smile that was almost tender. And to his surprise and pleasure she leaned up to press her lips against his cheek.

Always one to seize an opportunity, Quincannon gathered her into his arms and kissed her soundly on the mouth. At first, she struggled, then, for a few seconds, she softened and returned the kiss. Only for a few seconds, but a distinctly passionate few they were.

Sabina pushed him away and stepped back. Her cheeks were flushed. She fanned herself with one hand. A little breathlessly she said: "Good night, Mister Quincannon."

"Good night, my dear."

He stepped into the hallway. "You can just forget any notions that kiss may have given you," she said then. "It . . .

53

wasn't me who responded. It was the Saint Louis Rose."

Quincannon stood grinning as the door closed between them. *The Saint Louis Rose, indeed,* he thought.

And then he thought: *Oh, that Rose!*

Hero

The mob boiled upstreet from Saloon Row toward the jail-house. Some of the men in front carried lanterns and torches made out of rag-wrapped sticks soaked in coal oil. Micah could see the flickering light against the black night sky, the wild quivering shadows. But he couldn't see the men themselves, the hooded and masked leaders, from back here where he was at the rear of the pack. He couldn't see Ike Dall, either. Ike Dall was the one who had the hang rope already shaped into a noose.

Men surged around Micah, yelling, waving arms and clubs and six-guns. He just couldn't keep up on account of his damned game leg. He kept getting jostled, once almost knocked down. Back there at Hardesty's Gambling Hall he'd been right in the thick of it. He'd been the center of attention, by grab. Now they'd forgot all about him, and here he was clumping along on his bad leg, not able to see much, getting bumped and pushed with every dragging step. He could feel the excitement, smell the sweat and the heat and the hunger, but he wasn't a part of it any more.

It wasn't right. Hell damn boy, it just wasn't right. Weren't for him, none of this would be happening. Biggest damned thing ever in Cricklewood, Montana, and all on account of him. He was a hero, wasn't he? Back there at Hardesty's, they'd all said so. Back there at Hardesty's, he'd talked and they'd listened to every word—Ike Dall and Lee Wynkoop and Mack Clausen, all of them, everybody who was somebody in and around Cricklewood. Stood him right up there next to the bar, bought him drinks, looked at him with respect, and listened to every word he said.

"*Micah seen it, didn't you, Micah? What that drifter done?*"

"*Sure I did. Told Marshal Thrall and I'm tellin' you. Weren't for me, he'd've got clean away.*"

"*You're a hero, Micah. By God you are.*"

"*Well, now, I guess I am.*"

"*Tell it again. Tell us how it was.*"

"*Sure. Sure I will. I seen it all.*"

"*What'd you see?*"

"*I seen that drifter, that Larrabee, hold up the Wells Fargo stage. I seen him shoot Tom Porter twice, shoot Tom Porter dead as anybody ever was.*"

"*How'd you come to be out by the Helena road?*"

"*Mister Coombs sent me out from the livery to tell Harv Perkins the singletree on his wagon was fixed a day early. I took the shortcut along the river, like I allus do when I'm headin' down the valley. Forded by Fisherman's Bend and went on through that stand of cottonwoods on the other side. That was where I was, in them trees, when I seen it happen.*"

"*Larrabee had the stage stopped right there, did he?*"

"*Sure. Right there. Had his six-gun out and he was tellin' Tom to throw down the treasure box.*"

"*And Tom throwed it down?*"

"*Sure he did. He throwed it right down.*"

"*Never made to use his shotgun or his side gun?*"

"*No, sir. Never made no play at all.*"

"*So Larrabee shot him in cold blood.*"

"*Cold blood . . . sure! Shot Tom twice. Right off the coach box the first time, then, when Tom was lyin' there on the ground, rollin' around with that first bullet in him, Larrabee walked up to him cool as you please and put his six-gun ag'in' Tom's head and done it to him proper. Blowed Tom's head half off. Blowed it half off and that's a fact."*

"You all heard that. You heard what Micah seen that son-of-a-bitch do to Tom Porter . . . a decent citizen, a man we all liked and was proud to call friend. I say we don't wait for the circuit judge. What if he lets Larrabee off light? I say we give that murderin' bastard what he deserves here and now, tonight. Now what do you say?"

"Hang him!"

"Stretch his dirty neck!"

"Hang him high!"

Oh, it had been fine back there at Hardesty's. Everybody looking at him the way they done, with respect. Calling him a hero. He'd been somebody then, not just poor, crippled-up Micah Hays who'd done handy work and run errands and shoveled manure down at the Coombs Livery Barn. Oh, it had been fine! But now—now they'd forgot him again, left him behind, left him out of what was going to happen on *his* account. They were all moving upstreet to the jailhouse with their lanterns and their torches and their hunger, leaving him practically alone where he couldn't do or see a damned thing.

Micah stopped trying to run on his game leg and limped along, slow, watching the mob, wanting to be a part of it, but wanting more to see everything that happened after the mob got to the jailhouse. Then he thought: *Why, I can see it all! Sure I can! I know just where I got to go.*

He hobbled ahead to the alley alongside Burley's Feed and Grain, went down it to the staircase built up the side wall. The stairs led to a railed gallery overlooking the street, and to the top of the feed store roof. Micah stumped up the stairs and went past the dark offices and on down to the far end of the gallery.

Hell damn boy! He sure *could* see from up here, clear as

anybody could want. The mob was close to the jailhouse now. In the dancing light from the lanterns and torches, he could make out the hooded shape of Ike Dall with his hang-rope noose held high, the shapes of Lee Wynkoop and Mack Clausen and the others who were leading the pack. He could see that big old shade cottonwood off to one side of the jail, too, with its one gnarly limb that stretched out over the street. That was where they was going to hang the drifter. Ike Dall had said so back there at Hardesty's. *"We don't have to take him far, by Christ. We'll string him up right there next to the jail."*

The front door of the jailhouse opened and out come Marshal Thrall and his deputy, Ben Dietrich. Micah leaned out over the railing, squinting, feeling the excitement scurry up and down inside his chest like a mouse on a wall. Marshal Thrall had a shotgun in his hands, and Ben Dietrich held a rifle. The marshal commenced to yelling, but whatever it was got lost in the noise from the mob. Mob didn't slow down none, either, when old Thrall started waving that Greener of his. Marshal wasn't going to shoot nobody, Ike Dall had said. *"Why, we're all Thrall's friends and neighbors. Ben Dietrich's, too. They ain't goin' to shoot up their friends and neighbors, are they? Just to stop the lynching of a murderin' son-of-a-bitch like Larrabee?"*

No, sir, they sure wasn't. That mob didn't slow down none at all. It surged right ahead, right on around Marshal Thrall and Ben Dietrich like floodwaters around a sandbar, and swallowed them both up and carried them right on into the jailhouse.

A hell of a racket come from inside. Pretty soon the pack parted down the middle, and Micah could see four or five men carrying that drifter up in the air, hands tied behind him, the same way you'd carry a side of butchered beef. Hell damn boy! Everybody was whooping it up, waving torches and lanterns and twirling light around in the dark like a bunch of kids with pinwheel sparklers. It put Micah in mind of an Independence Day celebration. By grab, that was just what it was like. Fireworks on the Fourth of July.

Well, they carried that murdering Larrabee on over to the shade cottonwood. He was screaming things, that drifter was—screaming the whole way. Micah couldn't hear most of it above the crowd noise, but he caught a few of the words. And one whole sentence: "I tell you, I didn't do it!"

"Why, sure you did," Micah said out loud. "Sure you did. I seen you do it, didn't I?"

Ike Dall threw his rope over the cottonwood's gnarly limb, caught the other end, and gave it to somebody, and then he put that noose around Larrabee's neck and drew it tight. Somebody else brought a saddle horse around, held him steady whilst they hoisted the drifter onto his back. That Larrabee was screaming like a woman now.

Micah leaned hard against the gallery railing. His mouth was dry, real dry. He couldn't even work up no spit to wet it. He'd never seen a lynching before. There'd been plenty in Montana Territory—more'n a dozen over in Beaverhead and Madison counties a few years back, when the vigilantes done for Henry Plummer and his gang of desperadoes—but never one in Cricklewood or any of the other towns Micah had lived in.

The drifter screamed and screamed. Then Micah saw everybody back off some, away from the horse Larrabee was on, and Ike Dall raised his arm and brought it down smack on the cayuse's rump. The horse jumped ahead, frog-stepping, and Larrabee quit screaming and commenced to dancing in the air all loosey-goosey, like a puppet on the end of a string. Before long, though, the dancing slowed down, and then it quit altogether. *That's done him,* Micah thought. And everybody in the mob knew it, too, because they all backed off some more and stood there in a half circle, staring up at the drifter hanging still and straight in the smoky light.

Micah stared, too. He leaned against the railing and stared and stared, and kept on staring long after the mob started to break up.

Hell damn boy, he thought over and over. Hell damn boy, if that sure wasn't something to see!

It took the best part of a week for the town to get back to normal. There was plenty more excitement during that week—county law coming in, representatives from the territorial governor's office in Helena, newspaper people, all kinds of curious strangers. For Micah it was kind of like the lynching went on and on, a week-long celebration like none other he'd ever been part of. Folks kept asking him questions, interviewing him for newspapers, buying him drinks, shaking his hand and clapping his back and calling him a hero the way the men had done that night at Hardesty's. Oh, it was fine. It was almost as fine as when he'd been the center of attention before the lynch mob got started.

But then it all came to an end. The law and the newspaper people and the strangers went away. Cricklewood settled down to what it had been before the big event, and Micah settled back into his humdrum job at the Coombs Livery Barn and his handy work, running errands, shoveling manure— and the townsfolk and ranchers and cowhands stopped buying him drinks, stopped shaking his hand and clapping his back and calling him hero, stopped paying much attention to him at all. It was the same as before, like he was nobody, like he didn't hardly even exist. Mack Clausen snubbed him on the street no more than two weeks after the lynching. The one time he tried to get Ike Dall to talk with him about that night, how it had felt putting the noose around Larrabee's neck, Ike wouldn't have any of it. Why, Ike claimed, he hadn't even been there that night, hadn't been part of the mob—said that lie right to Micah's face!

Four weeks passed. Five. Micah did his handy work and ran errands and shoveled manure, and now nobody even mentioned that night any more, not to him and not to each other. Like it never happened. Like they were ashamed of it or something.

Micah was feeling low the hot Saturday morning he came down the loft ladder and started toward the harness room like he always did, first thing. But this wasn't like other mornings, because a man was curled up sleeping in one of the stalls near the back doors. Big man, whiskers on his face, dust on his trail clothes. Micah had never seen him before.

Mr. Coombs was up at the other end of the barn, forking hay for the two roan saddle horses he kept for rent. Micah went on up there and said: " 'Morning, Mister Coombs."

"Well, Micah. Down late again, eh?"

"I reckon so."

"Getting to be a habit lately," Mr. Coombs said. "I don't like it, Micah. See that you start coming down on time from now on, hear?"

"Yes, sir. Mister Coombs, who's that sleepin' in the back stall?"

"Just some drifter. He didn't say his name."

"Drifter?"

"Came in half drunk last night, paid me four bits to let him sleep in here. Not the first time I've rented out a stall to a human animal and it won't be the last."

Mr. Coombs turned and started forking some more hay. Micah went away toward the harness room, then stopped after ten paces and stood quiet for a space. And then, moving slowly, he hobbled over to where the fire axe hung and pulled it down and limped back behind Mr. Coombs and swung the axe up and shut his eyes and swung the axe down. When he opened his eyes again, Mr. Coombs was lying there with the back of his head cleaved open and blood and brains spilled out like pulp out of a split melon.

Hell damn boy, Micah thought.

Then he dropped the axe and ran to the front doors and threw them open and ran out onto Main Street, yelling at the top of his voice: "Murder! It's murder! Some damn' drifter killed Mister Coombs! Split his head wide open with a fire axe. I seen him do it, I seen it. I seen the whole thing!"

Doc Christmas, Painless Dentist

Nothing much happens in an eastern Montana farm and cow town like Bear Paw, even in the good warm days of early summer. So when this gent Doc Christmas and his assistant come rolling into town in their fancy wagon one fine June evening, unexpected and unannounced, it caused quite a commotion.

I was in the sheriff's office, where I conduct most of my civic business, when the hubbub commenced. I hurried out like everybody else to see what it was all about. First thing I saw was the wagon. It was a big, wide John Deere drawn by two bays and painted bright red with a shiny gold curlicue design. Smack in the middle of the design were the words: **DOC CHRISTMAS, PAINLESS DENTIST**. Then I saw up on the seat two of the oddest-looking gents a body was ever likely to set eyes on. The one holding the reins was four or five inches over six foot, beanpole thin, with a head as big as a melon and chin whiskers all the way down the front of his black broadcloth suit coat. The other one, wearing a mustard-yellow outfit, was half as tall, four times as wide, and bald as an egg, and he was strumming an outlandish big banjo and singing "Buffalo Gals" in a voice loud enough to dislodge rocks from Jawbone Hill.

Well, we'd had our fair share of patent medicine drummers in Bear Paw, and once we'd even had a traveling medicine show that had a juggler and twelve trained dogs and sold an herb compound and catarrh cure that give everybody that took it the trots. But we'd never had a painless dentist before.

Fact was, I'd never heard of this Doc Christmas. Turned out nobody else had, neither. He was brand-spanking new on the circuit, and that made him all the more of a curiosity. He drove that gaudy wagon of his straight down Main Street and across the river bridge, with half the townsfolk trailing after him like them German citizens trailed after the Pied Piper. Not just kids—men and women, too. And I ain't ashamed to admit that one of the men was yours truly, Randolph Tucker, sheriff and mayor of Bear Paw.

Doc Christmas parked his wagon on the willow flat along the river, with its hind end aimed out toward the road. It was getting on toward dusk by then, so him and the bald gent, whose name come out to be Homer, lighted pan torches that was tied to the wheels of the wagon. Then they opened up the back end and fiddled around until they had a kind of little stage with a painted curtain behind it. Then they got up on the stage part together, and Homer played more tunes on his banjo while the two of 'em sang the words, all louder than they was melodious. Then Doc Christmas begun setting out a display of dentist's instruments, on a slant-board table so the torchlight gleamed off their polished surfaces, and Homer went around handing out penny candy to the kids and printed leaflets to the adults.

I contrived to lay hands on one of the leaflets. It said that Doc Christmas was Montana Territory's newest and finest painless dentist, thanks be to his recent invention of Doc Christmas's Wonder Pain-Killer, **the most precious boon to mankind yet discovered**. It said he had dedicated his life to dispensing this fantastic new elixir, and to ridding the mouths of every citizen of Montana of loose and decayed teeth so's the rest of their teeth could remain healthy and harmonious. And at the very last it said what his services was going to cost you. Pint bottle of Doc Christmas's Wonder Pain-Killer, **a three months' supply with judicious use**—one dollar. A complete and thorough dental examination in his private clinic—four bits for adults, children under the age of ten free. Pulling of a loose or decayed tooth—one dollar for a simple extraction, three dollars for a difficult extraction that required more than five minutes. There was no other fees, and painless results was guaranteed to all.

As soon as the Doc had his instruments all laid out, Homer played a tune on his banjo to quieten everybody down. After which Doc Christmas began his lecture. It was some impressive. He said pretty much the same things his leaflet said, only in words so eloquent any politician would've been proud to steal 'em for his own.

Then he said he was willing to demonstrate the fabulous power of his pain-killer as a public service without cost to the first suffering citizen who volunteered to have a tooth drawn. Was there any poor soul here who had an aching molar or throbbing bicuspid? Doc Christmas invited him or her to step right up and be relieved.

Well, I figured it might take more than that for the doc to get himself a customer, even one for free. Folks in Bear Paw is just natural reticent when it comes to strangers and newfangled pain-killers, particular after the traveling medicine show's catarrh cure. But I was wrong. His offer was took up then and there by *two* citizens, not just one.

The first to speak up was Ned Flowers, who owns the feed and grain store. He was standing close in front, and no sooner had the doc finished his invite than Ned shouted: "I volunteer! I've got a side molar that's been giving me conniption fits for near a month."

"Step up here with me, sir," Doc Christmas said, "right up here with Homer and me."

Ned got one foot on the wagon, but not the second. There was a sudden roar, and somebody come barreling through the crowd like a bull on the scent of nine heifers, scattering bodies every which way. I knowed who it was even before I saw him and heard his voice boom out. "No you don't, Flowers! I got me a worse toothache than you or any man in sixteen counties. I'm gettin' my molar yanked first and I'm gettin' it yanked free and I ain't takin' argument from you nor nobody else!"

Elrod Patch. Bear Paw's blacksmith and bully, the meanest gent I ever had the misfortune to know personal. I'd arrested him six times in seven years, on charges from drunk and disorderly to cheating customers to assault and battery to caving in the skull of Abe Coltrane's stud Appaloosa when it kicked him whilst he was trying to shoe it, and I could've arrested him a dozen more times if I'd had enough evidence. He belonged in Deer Lodge Penitentiary, but he'd never been convicted of a felony offense, nor even spent more than a few days in my jail. Offended parties and witnesses had a peculiar way of dropping their complaints and changing their testimony when it come time to face the circuit judge.

Patch charged right up to the doc's wagon and shoved Ned outen the way and knocked him down, even though Ned wasn't fixing to argue. Then he clumb up on the stage, making the boards creak and groan and sag some. He was big, Patch was, muscle and fat both, with a wild tangle of red hair and a red mustache. He stood with his feet planted wide and looked hard at Doc Christmas. He'd been even meaner than usual lately, and now we all knew why.

"All right, sawbones," he said. "Pick up your tools and start yankin'."

"I am not a doctor, sir. I am a painless dentist."

"Same thing to me. Where do I sit?"

The doc fluffed out his whiskers and said: "The other gentleman volunteered first, Mister . . . ?"

"Patch, Elrod Patch, and I don't care if half of Bear Paw volunteered first. I'm here, and I'm the one sufferin' the worst. Get to it. And it damn' well better be painless, too."

I could've gone up there and stepped in on Ned Flowers's behalf, but it would've meant trouble, and I wasn't up to any trouble tonight if it could be avoided. Doc Christmas didn't want none, either. He said to Patch—"Very well, sir."—and made a signal to his assistant. Homer went behind the painted curtain, come out again with a chair like a cut-down barber's chair with a long horizontal rod at the top. He plunked the chair down next to the table that held the doc's instruments. Then he lighted the lantern and hooked it on the end of the rod.

Patch squeezed his bulk into the chair. The doc opened up Patch's mouth with one long-fingered hand, poked and prodded some inside, then went out and got a funny-looking tool and poked and prodded with that. He done it real gentle, too. Patch squirmed some, but never made a sound the whole time.

Homer come over with a bottle of Doc Christmas's Wonder Pain-Killer, and the doc held it up to show the crowd whilst he done some more orating on its virtues. After which he unstoppered it and swabbed some thick brown liquid on Patch's jaw, and rubbed more of it inside of Patch's mouth. When he was done, Homer handed him a pair of forceps, which the doc brandished for the assemblage. That pain-killer of his sure looked to be doing what it was advertised to do, for Patch was sitting quiet in the chair with a less hostile look on his ugly face.

He wasn't quiet for long, though. All of a sudden Homer took up his banjo and commenced to play and sing "Camptown Races" real loud. And with more strength than I'd figured was in that beanpole frame, Doc Christmas grabbed old Patch around the head with his hand tight over the windpipe, shoved the forceps into his wide-open maw, got him a grip on the offending molar, and started yanking.

It looked to me like Patch must be yelling something fierce. Leastways his legs was kicking and his arms was flapping. But Homer's banjo playing and singing was too loud to hear anything else. The doc yanked, and Patch struggled for what must've been about a minute and a half. Then the doc let go of his windpipe and with a flourish he held up the forceps, at the end of which was Patch's bloody tooth.

Patch tried to get up outen the chair. Doc Christmas shoved him back down, took a big wad of cotton off the table, and poked that into Patch's maw. Right then Homer quit picking and caterwauling. As soon as it was quiet, the doc said to the crowd: "A simple, painless extraction, ladies and gentlemen, accomplished in less time than it takes to peel and core an apple. It was painless, was it not, Mister Patch?"

Patch was on his feet now. He was wobbly, and he seemed a mite dazed. He tried to say something, but with all that cotton in his mouth the words come out garbled and thick, so's you couldn't understand none of 'em. Homer and the doc handed him down off the wagon. The townsfolk parted fast as Patch weaved his way through, giving him plenty of room. He passed close to me on his way out to the road, and he looked some stunned, for a fact. Whatever was in Doc Christmas's Wonder Pain-Killer sure must be a marvel of medical science.

Well, as soon as folks saw that Patch wasn't going to kick up a ruckus, they applauded Doc and Homer and pushed in closer to the wagon. In the next half hour, Doc Christmas pulled Ned Flowers's bad tooth and give a dozen four-bit dental examinations, and Homer sold nineteen bottles of the pain-killer. I bought a pint myself. I figured it was the least I could do in appreciation for the show they'd put on and that stunned look on Patch's face when he passed me by.

★ ★ ★ ★ ★

I was in my office early next morning, studying on the city council's proposal to buy fireworks from an outfit in Helena for this year's Fourth of July celebration, when Doc Christmas and Homer walked in. Surprised me to see 'em, particular since Homer looked some vexed. Not the doc, though. He'd struck me as the practical and unflappable sort last night, and he struck me the same in the light of day.

"Sheriff," he said, fluffing out his whiskers, "I wish to make a complaint."

"That so? What kind of complaint?"

"One of the citizens of Bear Paw threatened my life not twenty minutes ago. Homer's life, as well."

Uh-oh, I thought. "Wouldn't be Elrod Patch, would it?"

"It would. The man is a philistine."

"Won't get no argument from me on that," I said. "Philistine, troublemaker, and holy terror. What'd he threaten you and Homer for? Body'd think he'd be grateful, after you jerked his bad tooth free of charge."

"He claims it was not the painless extraction I guaranteed."

"Oh, he does."

"Claims to have suffered grievously the whole night long," Doc Christmas said, "and to still be in severe pain this morning. I explained to him that some discomfort is natural after an extraction, and that, if he had paid heed to my lecture, he would have understood the necessity of purchasing an entire bottle of Doc Christmas's Wonder Pain-Killer. Had he done so, he would have slept like an innocent babe and be fit as a fiddle today."

"What'd he say to that?"

"He insisted that I should have supplied a bottle of my Wonder Pain-Killer *gratis.* I informed him again that only the

69

public extraction was *gratis,* but he refused to listen."

"Just one of his many faults."

"He demanded a free bottle then and there. Of course, I did not knuckle under to such blatant extortion."

"That when he threatened your life?"

"In foul and abusive language."

"Uhn-huh. Any witnesses?"

"No, sir. We three were alone at the wagon."

"Well, then, sir," I said, "there just ain't much I can do legally. I don't know what to tell you gents, except that so far as I know Patch ain't never killed anybody human. So the chances are he won't follow up on his threat."

"But he would go so far as to damage my wagon and equipment, would he not?"

"He might, if he was riled enough. He threaten to do that, too?"

"He did."

"Hell and damn. I'll have to talk with him, Doc, try to settle him down. But he don't like me, and I don't like him, so I don't expect it'll do much good. How long you and Homer fixing to stay on in Bear Paw?"

"Business was brisk last evening," the doc said. "We anticipate it will be likewise today and tomorrow as well, once word spreads of my dental skill and the stupendous properties of Doc Christmas's Wonder Pain-Killer."

"I don't suppose you'd consider cutting your visit short and moving on elsewhere?"

He drew himself up. "I would not, sir. Doc Christmas flees before the wrath of no man."

"I was afraid of that. Uh, how long you reckon Patch's mouth will hurt without he treats it with more of your Wonder Pain-Killer?"

"The exact length of time varies from patient to patient. A

day, two days, perhaps as long as a week."

I sighed. "I was afraid of that, too."

Patch was banging away at a red-hot horseshoe with his five-pound sledge-hammer when I walked into his blacksmith's shop. Doing it with a vengeance, too, as if it was Doc Christmas's head forked there on his anvil. The whole left side of his face was swelled up something wicked.

He glared when he saw me. "What in hell do you want, Tucker?"

"A few peaceable words, is all."

"Got nothin' to say to you. Besides, my mouth hurts too damn' much to talk." Then, Patch being Patch, he went ahead and jawed to me anyways. "Look at what that travelin' tooth puller done to me last night. Hurts twice as bad with the tooth out than it done with it in."

"Well, you did rush up and volunteer to have it yanked."

"I didn't volunteer for no swole-up face like I got now. Painless dentist, hell!"

"It's my understanding you threatened him and his assistant with bodily harm."

"Run to you, did he?" Patch said. "Well, it'd serve both of 'em right if I blowed their heads off with my Twelve-Gauge."

"You'd hang, Patch. High and quick."

He tried to scowl, but it hurt his face, and he winced instead. He give the horseshoe another lick with his hammer, then dropped it into a bucket of water. He watched it steam and sizzle before he said: "There's other ways to skin a cat."

"Meaning?"

"Like I said. They's other ways to skin a cat."

"Patch, you listen to me. You do anything to Doc Christmas or Homer or that wagon of theirs, anything at all, I'll slap you in jail sudden and see that you pay dear."

"I ain't afraid of you, Tucker. You and me's gonna tangle one of these days anyhow."

"Better not, if you know what's good for you."

"I know what's good for me right now, and that's some of that bastard's pain-killer. It's the genuine article, even if he ain't. And I aim to get me a bottle."

"Now, that's the first sensible thing I heard you say. Whyn't you and me mosey on down to the river together so's you can buy one?"

"Buy? I ain't gonna *buy* somethin' I should've got for nothin'!"

"Oh, Lordy, Patch. Doc Christmas never promised you a free bottle of pain-killer. All he promised was to draw your bad tooth, which he done."

"One's free, so's the other," Patch said. "Ain't nobody cheats Elrod Patch outen what's rightfully his and gets away with it. Sure not the flim-flammin' long drink of water that claims to be a painless dentist."

Well, it just wasn't no use. I'd have got more satisfaction trying to talk sense to a cottonwood stump. But I give it one last try before I took myself out of there. I said: "You're warned, mister. Stay away from Doc Christmas and Homer and their wagon or you'll suffer worse'n you are now by half. And that's a promise."

All I got for an answer was a snort. He was on his way to the forge by then, else I reckon he'd have laughed right in my face.

Long about noonday I had an inspiration.

I walked home to Madge Tolliver's boarding house for my noon meal, which I like to do as often as I can on account of Madge being the best cook in town, and afterwards I went upstairs to my room for the bottle of Doc Christmas's Wonder Pain-Killer I'd bought last night. Outside again, I spied the

Ames boy, Tommy, rolling his hoop. I gave Tommy a nickel
to take the bottle to the blacksmith's shop. I said he should
tell Patch it was from Doc Christmas and that it was a peace
offering, free of charge. I don't like fibbing or having young-
sters fib for me, but in this case I reckoned I was on the side of
the angels and it was a pardonable sin. Sometimes the only
way you can deal with the devil is by using his own methods.

I waited fifteen minutes for Tommy to come back. When
he did, he didn't have the bottle of pain-killer with him,
which I took to be a good sign. But it wasn't.

"He took it all right, Mister Tucker," Tommy said. "Then
he laughed real nasty and said he suspicioned it was from you,
not Doc Christmas."

"Blast him for a sly fox!"

"He said now he had *two* bottles of pain-killer, and his
mouth didn't hurt no more, but it didn't make a lick of difference in how he felt toward that blankety-blank tooth puller."

"Two bottles?"

"Got the other one from Mister Flowers, he said."

"By coercion, I'll warrant."

"What's coercion?"

"Never you mind about that. Patch didn't say what he was
fixing to do about Doc Christmas, did he?"

"No, sir, he sure didn't."

I left Tommy and stumped on down to the river to see the
doc. There was a crowd around his wagon again, not as large
today, but still good-sized. Doc had a farmer in the chair and
was yanking a tooth while Homer played his banjo and sang
"Camptown Races." I waited until they was done and eight
more bottles of the Wonder Pain-Killer had been sold. Then I
got the Doc off to one side for a confab.

I told him what Patch had said to me and to Tommy
Ames. I thought it might scare him some, but it didn't. He

drew himself up the way he liked to do, fluffed his whiskers, and said: "Homer and I refuse to be intimidated by the likes of Elrod Patch."

"He can be mean, Doc, and that's a fact. He's as likely as a visit from the Grim Reaper to make trouble for you."

"Be that as it may."

"Doc, I'd take it as a personal favor if you'd pull up stakes and move on right now. By the time you make your circuit back to Bear Paw, Patch'll have forgot his grudge. . . ."

"I'm sorry, Sheriff Tucker, but that would be the cowardly way, and Homer and I are men, not spineless whelps. The law and the Almighty can send us fleeing, but no man can without just cause."

Well, he had a point, and I couldn't argue with it. He was on public land, and he hadn't broken any laws, including the Almighty's. I wished him well and went back to town.

But I was feeling uneasy in my mind and tight in my bones. There was going to be trouble, sure as God made little green apples, and now I couldn't see no smart nor legal way to stop it.

It happened some past midnight, and, depending on how you looked at it, it was plain trouble or trouble with a fitting end and a silver lining. Most if not all of Bear Paw looked at it the second way. And I'd be a hypocrite if I said I wasn't one of the majority.

I was sound asleep when the knocking commenced on the door to my room at the boarding house. I lighted my lamp before I opened up. It was Doc Christmas, looking as unflappable as ever.

First thing he done was unbutton his frock coat and hand me a pistol, butt first, that had been tucked into his belt. It was an old Root's Patent Model .31 caliber with a side hammer like a musket hammer, a weapon I hadn't seen in many a year. But it looked to be in fine working order, and the barrel was warm.

"Sheriff," he said then, "I wish to report a shooting."

"Who got shot?"

"Elrod Patch."

"Oh, Lordy. Is he dead?"

"As the proverbial doornail."

"You the one who shot him?"

"I am. In self-defense."

He might've been telling me the time of night—he was that calm and matter-of-fact. Practical to a fault, that was the doc. What was done was done, and there wasn't no sense in getting exercised about it.

I asked him: "Where'd it happen?"

"On the willow flat near where my wagon is parked. Homer is waiting there for us. Shall we proceed?"

I got dressed in a hurry, and we hustled on down to the river. Homer was tending to one of the bay horses, both of which seemed unusual skittish. Nearby, between where the horses was picketed and the wagon, Elrod Patch lay sprawled out on his back. In one hand he held a five-pound sledgehammer, of all things, and there was a bullet hole where he'd once had a right eye.

"It was unavoidable, Sheriff," Homer said as I bent to look at Patch. "He rushed at the doc with that hammer and left him no choice."

"What in tarnation was Patch doing here with a sledgehammer? Not attempting to murder you gents in your beds, was he?"

"No," Doc Christmas said. "He was attempting to murder our horses."

"Your horses?"

"It was their frightened cries that woke Homer and me. Fortunately we emerged from the wagon before he had time to do more than strike one of the animals a glancing blow."

Well, I knew right then that the Doc and Homer was telling the truth. Patch had caved in the skull of Abe Coltrane's stud Appaloosa with nary a qualm nor regret, and I could see where doing the same to a couple of wagon horses would be just his idea of revenge. Still, I had my duty. I looked close at the sledge-hammer to make sure it was Patch's. It was. His initials was cut into the handle. Then I examined the bay that had been struck and found a bloody mark across his neck and withers. That was enough for me.

"Self-defense and death by misadventure," I said, and I give the doc back his .31 Root's. "Patch had it coming . . . no mistake about that, neither. Too bad you had to be the one to send him to his reward, Doc."

He said—"Yes."—but he looked kind of thoughtful when he said it.

Doc Christmas come to see me one more time, late the following afternoon at my office. At first I thought it was just to tell me him and Homer was leaving soon for Sayersville. Then I thought it was to ask if they'd be welcome back when Bear Paw come up on their circuit again next spring, which I said they would be. But them two things was only preambles to the real purpose of his visit.

"Sheriff Tucker," he said, "it is my understanding that you are also the mayor and city treasurer of Bear Paw. Is this correct?"

"It is," I said. "I'm likewise chairman of the annual Fourth of July celebration and head of the burial commission. Folks figured it was better to pay one man a salary for wearing lots of hats than a bunch of men salaries for wearing one hat apiece."

"Then you are empowered to pay out public funds for services to the community."

"I am. What're you getting at, Doc?"

"The fact," he said, "that Bear Paw owes me three dollars."

"Bear Paw does what? What in tarnation for?"

"Services rendered."

"Come again?"

"Services rendered," the doc said. "I am a painless dentist, as you well know . . . the finest and most dedicated painless dentist in Montana Territory. It is my life's work and my duty and my great joy to rid the mouths of my patients of loose and decayed teeth. A town such as Bear Paw, sir, is in many ways like the mouth of one of my patients. It is healthy and harmonious only so long as its citizens . . . its individual teeth, if you will . . . are each and every one healthy and harmonious. One diseased tooth damages the entire mouth. Elrod Patch was such a diseased tooth in the mouth of Bear Paw. I did not extract him willingly from your midst, but the fact remains that I did extract him permanently . . . and with no harm whatsoever to the surrounding teeth. In effect, sir, painlessly.

"For a simple painless extraction I charge one dollar. You will agree, Sheriff Tucker, that the extraction of Elrod Patch was not simple, but difficult. For difficult extractions I charge three dollars. Therefore, the town of Bear Paw owes me three dollars for services rendered, payable on demand."

Did I say the doc was practical to a fault? And then some! He was a caution, he was, with more gall than a trainload of campaigning politicians. If I'd been a lawyer, I reckon I could've come up with a good argument against his claim.

But I ain't a lawyer, I'm a public servant. Besides which, when a man's right, he's right.

On behalf of the healthy and harmonious teeth of Bear Paw, I paid Doc Christmas his three dollars.

McIntosh's Chute

It was right after supper, and we were all settled around the cook fire, smoking, none of us saying much because it was well along in the roundup and we were all dog-tired from the long days of riding and chousing cows out of brush-clogged coulées. I wasn't doing anything except taking in the night—warm Montana fall night, sky all hazed with stars, no moon to speak of. Then, of a sudden, something come streaking across all that velvet-black and silver from east to west: a ball of smoky red-orange with a long fiery tail. Everybody stirred around and commenced to gawping and pointing. But not for long. Quick as it had come, the thing was gone beyond the broken saw-teeth of the Rockies.

There was a hush. Then young Poley said: "What in hell was *that?*" He was just eighteen and big for his britches in more ways than one. But that heavenly fireball had taken him down to an awed whisper.

"Comet," Cass Buckram said.

"That fire-tail . . . *whooee!*" Poley said. "I never seen nothing like it. Comet, eh? Well, it's the damnedest sight a man ever set eyes on."

"Damnedest sight a *button* ever set eyes on, maybe."

"I ain't a button!"

"You are from where I sit," Cass said. "Big shiny man-sized button with your threads still dangling."

Everybody laughed except Poley. Being as he was the youngest on the roundup crew, he'd taken his share of ragging since we'd left the Box B, and he was about fed up with it. He said: "Well, what do *you* know about it, old-timer?"

That didn't faze Cass. He was close to sixty, though you'd never know it to look at him or watch him when he worked cattle or at anything else, but age didn't mean much to him. He was of a philosophical turn of mind. You were what you were and no sense in pretending otherwise—that was how he looked at it.

In his younger days he'd been an adventuresome gent. Worked at jobs most of us wouldn't have tried in places we'd never even hoped to visit. Oil rigger in Texas and Oklahoma, logger in Oregon, fur trapper in the Canadian Barrens, prospector in the Yukon during the 1898 rush, cowhand in half a dozen states and territories. He'd packed more living into the past forty-odd years than a whole regiment of men, and he didn't mind talking about his experiences. No, he sure didn't mind. First time I met him, I'd taken him for a blowhard. Plenty took him that way in the beginning, on account of his windy nature. But the stories he told were true, or at least every one had a core of truth in it. He had too many facts and a whole war bag full of mementoes and photographs and such to back 'em up.

All you had to do was prime him a little—and without knowing it young Poley had primed him just now. But that was all right with the rest of us. Cass had honed his story-telling skills over the years; one of his yarns was always worth-while entertainment.

He said to the kid: "I saw more strange things before I was twenty than you'll ever see."

"Cowflop."

"Correct word is bullshit," Cass said, solemn, and every-body laughed again. "But neither one is accurate."

"I suppose you seen something strange and more spectac-ular than that there comet."

"Twice as strange and three times as spectacular."

"Cowflop."

"Fact. Ninth wonder of the world, in its way."

"Well? What was it?"

"McIntosh and his chute."

"Chute? What chute? Who was McIntosh?"

"Keep your lip buttoned, button, and I'll tell you. I'll tell you about the damnedest sight I or any other man ever laid eyes on.

"Happened more than twenty years ago," Cass went on, "in southern Oregon in the early 'Nineties. I'd had my fill of fur-trapping in the Barrens and developed a hankering to see what timber work was like, so I'd come on down into Oregon and hooked on with a logging outfit near Coos Bay. But for the first six months I was just a bullcook, not a timber jack. Low-down work, bullcooking . . . cleaning up after the 'jacks, making up their bunks, cutting firewood, helping out in the kitchen. Without experience, that's the only kind of job you can get in a decent logging camp. Boss finally put me on one of the yarding crews, but even then there was no thrill in the work, and the wages were low. So I was ready for a change of venue when word filtered in that a man named Saginaw Tom McIntosh was hiring for his camp on Black Mountain.

"McIntosh was from Michigan and had made a pile logging in the North Woods. What had brought him west to Oregon was the opportunity to buy better than twenty-five thousand acres of virgin timberland on Black Mountain. He'd rebuilt an old dam on the Klamath River nearby that been washed out by high water, built a sawmill and a millpond below the dam, and then started a settlement there that he named after himself. And once he had a camp operating on the mountain, first thing he did was construct a chute, or skidway, down to the river.

"Word of McIntosh's chute spread just as fast and far as word that he was hiring timber beasts at princely wages. It was supposed to be an engineering marvel, unlike any other logging chute ever built. Some scoffed when they were told about it, claimed it was just one of those tall stories that get flung around among Northwest loggers, like the one about Paul Bunyan and Babe, the blue ox. Me, I was willing to give Saginaw Tom McIntosh the benefit of the doubt. I figured that if he was half the man he was talked of being, he could accomplish just about anything he set his mind to.

"He had two kinds of reputation. First, as a demon logger . . . a man who could get timber cut faster and turned into board lumber quicker than any other boss 'jack. And second, as a ruthless, cold-hearted son-of-a-bitch who bullied his men, worked them like animals, and wasn't above using fists, peaveys, calks, and any other handy weapon if the need arose. Rumor had it that he. . . .

"What's that, boy? No, I ain't going to say any more about that chute just yet. I'll get to it in good time. You just keep your pants on and let me tell this my own way.

"Well, rumor had it that McIntosh was offering top dollar because it was the only way he could get 'jacks to work steady for him. That and his reputation didn't bother me one way or another. I'd dealt with hardcases before, and have since. So I determined to see what Saginaw Tom and his chute and Black Mountain were all about.

"I quit the Coos Bay outfit and traveled down to McIntosh's settlement on the Klamath. Turned out to be bigger than I'd expected. The sawmill was twice the size of the one up at Coos Bay, and there was a blacksmith shop, a box factory, a hotel and half a dozen boarding houses, two big stores, a school, two churches, and a lodge hall. McIntosh may have been a son-of-a-bitch, but he sure did know how to get maximum production and how to provide for his men and their families.

"I hired on at the mill, and the next day a crew chief named Lars Nilson drove me and another new man, a youngster called Johnny Cline, upriver to the Black Mountain camp. Long, hot trip in the back of a buckboard, up steep grades and past gold-mining claims strung along the rough-water river. Nilson told us there was bad blood between McIntosh and those miners. They got gold out of the sand by trapping silt in wing dams, and they didn't like it when McIntosh's river drivers built holding cribs along the banks or herded long chains of logs downstream to the cribs and then on to the mill. There hadn't been any trouble yet, but it could erupt at any time. Feelings were running high on both sides.

"Heat and flies and hornets deviled us all the way up into the scrub timber . . . lodgepole, jack, and yellow pine. The bigger trees . . . white sugar pine . . . grew higher up, and what fine old trees they were. Clean-growing, hardly any underbrush. Huge trunks that rose up straight from brace roots close to four feet broad, and no branches on 'em until thirty to forty feet above the ground. Every lumberman's dream, the cut-log timber on that mountain.

"McIntosh was taking full advantage of it, too. His camp was twice the size of most . . . two enormous bunkhouses, a cook shack, a barn and blacksmith shop, clusters of sheds and shanties and heavy wagons, corrals full of work horses and oxen. Close to a hundred men, altogether. And better than two dozen big wheels, stinger-tongue and slip-tongue both. . . .

"What's a big wheel? Just that, boy . . . wheels ten and twelve feet high, some made of wood and some of iron, each pair connected by an axle that had a chain and a long tongue poking back from the middle. Four-horse team drew each one. Man on the wheel crew dug a shallow trench under one or two logs, depending on their size . . . loader pushed the chain through it under the logs and secured it to the axle . . . driver lunged his team ahead, and the tongue slid forward and yanked on the chain to lift the front end of the logs off the ground. Harder the horses pulled, the higher the logs hung. When the team came to a stop, the logs dropped and dragged. Only trouble was, sometimes they didn't drop and drag just right . . . didn't act as a brake like they were supposed to . . . and the wheel horses got their hind legs smashed. Much safer and faster to use a steam lokey to get logs out of the woods, but laying narrow gauge track takes time and so does ordering a lokey and having it packed in sections up the side of a wilderness mountain. McIntosh figured to have his track laid and a lokey operating by the following spring. Meanwhile, it was the big wheels and the teams of horses and oxen and men that had to do the heavy work.

"Now, then. The chute . . . McIntosh's chute.

"First I seen of it was across the breadth of the camp, at the edge of a steep drop-off . . . the chute head, a big two-level platform built of logs. Cut logs were stacked on the top level as they came off the big wheels by 'jacks crow-hopping over the deck with cant hooks. On the lower level other 'jacks looped a cable around the foremost log, and a donkey engine wound up the cable and hauled the log forward into a trough built at the outer edge of the platform. You follow me so far?

"Well, that was all I could see until Nilson took Johnny Cline over close to the chute head. From the edge of the drop-off you had a miles-wide view . . . long, snaky stretches of the Klamath, timberland all the way south to the California border. But it wasn't the vista that had my attention . . . it was the chute itself. An engineering marvel, all right, that near took my breath away.

"McIntosh and his crew had cut a channel in the rocky hillside straight on down to the riverbank, and lined the sides and bottom with flat-hewn logs . . . big ones at the sides and smaller ones on the bottom, all worn glass-smooth. Midway along was a kind of trestle that spanned an outcrop and acted as a speed-brake. Nothing legendary about that chute. It was the longest built up to that time, maybe the longest ever! More than twenty-six hundred feet of timber had gone into the construction, top to bottom.

"While I was gawking down at it, somebody shouted . . . 'Clear back!' . . . and right away Nilson herded Johnny Cline and me onto a hummock to one side. At the chute head a chain of logs was lined and ready, held back by an iron bar wedged into the rock. Far down below one of the river crew showed a white flag, and, as soon as he did, the chute tender yanked the iron bar aside, and the first log shuddered through and down.

"After a hundred feet or so, it began to pick up speed. You could hear it squealing against the sides and bottom of the trough. By the time it went over the trestle and into the lower part of the chute, it was a blur. Took just eighteen seconds for it to drop more than eight hundred feet to the river and, when it hit, the splash was bigger than a barn, and the fan of water drenched trees on both banks. . . ."

"Hell!" young Poley interrupted. "I don't believe none of that. You're funning us, Cass."

"Be damned if I am. What don't you believe?"

"None of it. Chute twenty-six hundred feet of timber, logs shooting down over eight hundred feet in less than twenty seconds, splashes bigger than a barn. . . ."

"Well, it's the gospel truth. So's the rest of it. Sides and bottom a third of the way down were burned black from the friction . . . black as coal. On cold mornings you could see smoke from the logs going down, that's how fast they traveled. Went even faster when there was frost, so the river crew had to drive spikes in the chute's bottom end to slow 'em up. Even so, sometimes a log would hit the river with enough force to split it in half, clean, like it'd gone through a buzz saw. But I expect you don't believe none of that, either."

Poley grunted. "Not hardly."

I said: "Well, *I* believe it, Cass. Man can do just about anything he sets his mind to, like you said, if he wants it bad enough. That chute must've been something. I can sure see why it was the damnedest thing you ever saw."

"No, it wasn't," Cass said.

"What? But you said. . . ."

"No, I didn't. McIntosh's chute was a wonder but not the damnedest thing I ever saw."

"Then what *is?*" Poley demanded.

"If I wasn't interrupted every few minutes, you'd've found out by now." Cass glared at him. "You going to be quiet and let me get to it, or you intend to keep flapping your gums so this here story takes all night?"

Poley wasn't cowed, but he did button his lip. And surprised us all—maybe even himself—by keeping it buttoned for the time being.

"I thought I might get put on one of the wheel crews," Cass resumed, "but I'd made the mistake of telling Nilson I'd worked a yarding crew up at Coos Bay, so a yarding crew was where I got put on Black Mountain. Working as a chokesetter in the slash out back of the camp . . . man that sets heavy cable chokers around the end of a log that's fallen down a hillside or into a ravine so the log can be hauled out by means of a donkey engine. Hard, sweaty, dangerous work in the best of camps, and McIntosh's was anything but the best. The runners had been right about that, too. We worked long hours for our pay, seven days a week. And if a man dropped from sheer exhaustion, he was expected to get up under his own power . . . and was docked for the time he spent lying down.

"Johnny Cline got put on the same crew, as a whistle-punk on the donkey, and him and me took up friendly. He was a Californian, from down near San Francisco, young and feisty and too smart-ass for his own good . . . some like you, Poley. But decent enough, underneath. His brother was a logger somewhere in Canada, and he'd determined to try his hand, too. He was about as green as me, but you could see that logging was in his blood in a way that it wasn't in mine. I knew I'd be moving on to other things one day. He knew he'd be a logger till the day he died.

"I got along with Nilson and most of the timber beasts, but Saginaw Tom McIntosh was another matter. If anything, he was worse than his reputation . . . man clear through, with about as much decency as a vulture on a fence post waiting for something to die. Giant of a man, face weathered the color of heartwood, droopy yellow mustache stained with juice from the quids of Spearhead tobacco he always kept stowed in one cheek, eyes like pale fire that gave you the feeling you'd been burned whenever they touched you. Stalked around camp in worn cruisers, stagged corduroy pants, and steel-calked boots, yelling out orders, knocking men down with his fists if they didn't ask how high when he hollered jump. Ran that camp the way a hard-ass warden runs a prison. Everybody hated him, including me and Johnny Cline before long. But most of the 'jacks feared him, too, which was how he kept them in line.

"He drove all his crews hard, demanding that a dozen

turns of logs go down his chute every day to feed the saws working twenty-four hours at the mill. Cut lumber was fetching more than a hundred dollars per thousand feet at the time, and he wanted to keep production at a fever pitch before the heavy winter rains set in. There was plenty of grumbling among the men, and tempers were short, but nobody quit the camp. Pay was too good, even with all the abuse that went along with it.

"I'd been at the Black Mountain camp three weeks when the real trouble started. One of the gold miners down on the Klamath, man named Coogan, got drunk and decided to tear up a holding crib because he blamed McIntosh for ruining his claim. McIntosh flew into a rage when he heard about it. He ranted and raved for half a day about how he'd had enough of those god-damn' miners. Then, when he'd worked himself up enough, he ordered a dozen 'jacks down on a night raid to bust up Coogan's wing dam and raise some hell with the other miners' claims. The 'jacks didn't want to do it, but he bullied them into it with threats and promises of bonus money.

"But the miners were expecting retaliation, had joined forces, and were waiting when the 'jacks showed up. There was a riverbank brawl, mostly with fists and axe handles, but with a few shots fired, too. Three timber stiffs were hurt bad enough so that they had to be carried back to camp and would be laid up for a while.

"The county law came next day and threatened to close McIntosh down if there was any more trouble. That threw him into another fit. Kind of man he was, he took it out on the men in the raiding party.

" 'What kind of 'jack lets a gold-grubber beat him down?' he yelled at them. "You buggers ain't worth the name timber jack. If I didn't need your hands and backs, I'd send the lot of you packing. As is, I'm cutting your pay. And you three that can't work . . . you get no pay at all until you can hoist your peaveys and swing your axes.'

"One of the 'jacks challenged him. McIntosh kicked the man in the crotch, knocked him down, and then gave him a case of logger's smallpox . . . pinned his right arm to the ground with those steel calks of his. There were no other challenges. But in all those bearded faces you could see the hate that was building for McIntosh. You could feel it, too. It was in the air, crackles of it like electricity in a storm.

"Another week went by. There was no more trouble with the miners, but McIntosh drove his crews with a vengeance. Up to fifteen turns of logs down the chute each day. The big-wheel crews hauling until their horses were ready to drop, and two did drop dead in harness, while another two had to be destroyed when logs crushed their hind legs on the drag. Buckers and fallers working the slash from dawn to dark, so that the skirl of crosscuts and bucksaws and the thud of axes rolled like constant thunder across the face of Black Mountain.

"Some men can stand that kind of killing pace without busting down one way or another, and some men can't. Johnny Cline was one of those who couldn't. He was hot-headed, like I said before, and ten times every day and twenty times every night he cursed McIntosh and damned his black soul. Then, one day when he'd had all he could swallow, he made the mistake of cursing and damning McIntosh to the boss logger's face.

"The yarding crew we were on was deep in the slash, struggling to get logs out of a small valley. It was coming on dusk, and we'd been at it for hours. We were all bone-tired. I set the choker around the end of yet another log, and the hook tender signaled Johnny Cline, who stood behind him with one hand on the wire running to the whistle on the donkey engine. When Johnny pulled the wire and the short blast sounded, the cable snapped tight, and the big log started to move, its nose plowing up dirt and crushing saplings in its path. But as it came up the slope, it struck a sunken log, as sometimes happens, and shied off. The hook-tender signaled for slack, but Johnny didn't give it fast enough to keep the log from burying its nose in the roots of a fir stump.

"McIntosh saw it. He'd come cat-footing up and was ten feet from the donkey engine. He ran up to Johnny yelling . . . 'You stupid god-damn' greenhorn!' . . . and gave him a shove that knocked the kid halfway down to where the log was stumped.

"Johnny caught himself and scrambled back up the incline. I could see the hate afire in his eyes, and I tried to get between him and McIntosh, but he brushed me aside. He put his face up close to the boss logger's, spat out a string of cuss words, and finished up with . . . 'I've had all I'm gonna take from you, you son-of-a-bitch.' And then he swung with his right hand.

"But all he hit was air. McIntosh had seen it coming. He stepped inside the punch and spat tobacco juice into Johnny's face. The squirt and spatter threw the kid off balance and blinded him at the same time . . . left him wide open for McIntosh to wade in with fists and knees.

"McIntosh seemed to go berserk, as if all the rage and meanness had built to an explosion point inside him, and Johnny's words had triggered it. Johnny Cline never had a chance. McIntosh beat him to the ground, kept on beating him even though me and some of the others fought to pull him off. And when he saw his chance, he raised up one leg, and he stomped the kid's face with his calks . . . drove those sharp steel spikes down into Johnny's face as if he was grinding a bug under his heel.

"Johnny screamed once, went stiff, then lay still. Nilson and some others had come running up by then, and it took six of us to drag McIntosh away before he could smallpox Johnny Cline a second time. He battled us for a few seconds, like a crazy man, then, all at once, the wildness went out of him. But he was no more human when it did. He tore himself loose, and without a word, without any concern for the boy he'd stomped, he stalked off through the slash.

"Johnny Cline's face was a red ruin, pitted and torn by half a hundred steel points. I thought he was dead at first, but when I got down beside him, I found a weak pulse. Four of us picked him up and carried him to our bunkhouse.

"The bullcook and me cleaned the blood off him and doctored his wounds as best we could. But he was in a bad way. His right eye was gone, pierced by one of McIntosh's calks, and he was hurt inside, too, for he kept coughing up red foam. There just wasn't much we could do for him. The nearest doctor was thirty miles away. By the time somebody went and fetched him back, it would be too late. I reckon we all knew from the first that Johnny Cline would be dead by morning.

"There was no more work for any of us that day. None of the 'jacks in our bunkhouse took any grub, either, nor slept much as the night wore on. We all just sat around in little groups with our lamps lit, talking low, smoking and drinking coffee or tea. Checking on Johnny now and then. Waiting.

"He never regained consciousness. An hour before dawn the bullcook went to look at him and announced . . . 'He's gone.' The waiting was done. Yes, and so were Saginaw Tom McIntosh and the Black Mountain camp.

"Nilson and the other crew chiefs had a meeting outside, between the two bunkhouses. The rest of us kept our places. When Nilson and the two others who bunked in our building came back in, it was plain enough from their expressions what had been decided. And plainer still when the three of them shouldered their peaveys. Loggers will take so much from a boss like Saginaw Tom McIntosh . . . only so much and no more. What he'd done to Johnny Cline was the next to last straw. Johnny dying was the final one.

"At the door Nilson said . . . 'We're on our way to cut down a rotted tree. Rest of you can stay on or join us, as you see fit. But you'll keep your mouths shut, either way. Clear?'

"Nobody had any objections. Nilson turned and went out with the other two chiefs.

"Well, none of the men in our bunkhouse stayed, nor did anybody in the other one. We were all of the same mind. I thought I knew what would happen to McIntosh, but I was wrong. The crew heads weren't fixing to give him the same as he gave Johnny Cline. No, they had other plans. When a logging crew turns, it turns hard . . . and it gives no quarter.

"The near-dawn dark was chill and damp, and I don't mind saying it put a shiver on my back. We all walked quiet through it to McIntosh's shanty . . . close to a hundred of us, so he heard us coming anyway. But not in time to get up a weapon. He fought with the same wildness he had earlier, but he didn't have any more chance than he gave Johnny Cline. Nilson stunned him with his peavey. Then half a dozen men stuffed him into his clothes and his blood-stained boots and took him out.

"Straight across the camp we went, with four of the crew heads carrying McIntosh by the arms and legs. He came around just before they got him to the edge of the drop-off. He realized what was going to happen to him, looked like, at about the same time I did.

"He was struggling fierce, bellowing curses, when Nilson and the others pitched him into the chute.

"He went down slow at first, the way one of the big logs always did. Clawing at the flat-hewn sides, trying to dig his calks into the glass-smooth bottom logs. Then he commenced to pick up speed, and his yells turned to banshee screams. Two hundred feet down the screaming stopped. He was just a blur by then. His clothes started to smoke from the friction, then burst into flame. When he went sailing over the trestle, he was a lump of fire that lit up the dark . . . then a streak of fire as he shot down into the lower section . . . then a fireball with a tail longer and brighter than the one on that comet a while ago, so bright the river and the woods on both sides showed plain as day for two or three seconds before he smacked the river . . . smacked it and went out in a splash and steamy sizzle you could see and hear all the way up at the chute head.

"And that," Cass Buckram finished, "*that,* by God, was the damnedest sight I or any other man ever set eyes on . . . McIntosh going down McIntosh's chute, eight hundred feet straight into hell."

None of us argued with him. Not even Poley, the button.

Fyfe and the Drummers

Old-time drummers was a peculiar bunch. It's a fact. I been tending bar here for near forty years—F. X. Fyfe, at your service—and I seen all sorts of folks come through New Appia and the New Appia Hotel, good and bad and some strange. But drummers back before the century turned . . . well, there just weren't none like them peckerwoods. Whisky drummers, cigar drummers, lightning-rod drummers, windmill drummers . . . they was *all* a caution.

You take their general appearance. Not one of them salesmen ever set out to dress like other folks. No, sir. They all wore fancy suits that might've been made of horse blankets, they was that flashy. And waistcoats in different colors than the suits, some decorated with flower patterns that set you in mind of window drapery. And stiff shirts and four-in-hand ties and stickpins with big fake jewels in 'em. And patent-leather shoes shined bright enough so's you could shave and comb your hair looking into the gloss. Most of 'em wore waxed mustaches, too, sometimes dyed pure black, with the ends so stiff and pointy you could've used one to pick your teeth.

Then there was what come out when them boys opened their mouths. Talk? Lordy, old-time drummers could talk a miser out of his gold, a girl out of her drawers, and a politician out of three bought votes. Charm by the carload, that's what they had, and weren't none of it any deeper than a skin of ice after the first hard freeze. Them peckerwoods didn't have to *work* at being salesmen; they was just natural-born liars and flim-flammers.

You think cowboys is hard drinkers? Why, they're pikers compared to drummers. More times than I can count I threw one out, put another to bed, and served 'em Fyfe's Own Hangover Cure on the morning after. You think Frenchmen is great lovers? I never seen a drummer that wasn't hell-on-wheels with the ladies—or thought he was, or pretended he was. You think minstrel-show and vaudeville comedians know a passel of comical stories? Why, drummers could tell stories for a week straight and never run out. Most of their jokes was bawdy, some was even funny, and danged if they couldn't make you laugh now and then at one that *wasn't* funny.

Yes, sir, all them old-timers was a caution. But I reckon the patent medicine peddlers was the most cock-eyed of the lot. How so? Well, I'll give you a first-class example.

This here happened back in the early 'Nineties. Late January, it was. Cold, raw night, mostly wind with a little sleet in it. Wasn't many guests registered at the hotel—never is, that time of year—and there was only half a dozen or so steady customers in the bar parlor when Charley Tuggle walked in.

Charley Tuggle had been a patent medicine drummer for half his forty years—to hear him tell it, anyhow. I knew him tolerable well on account of he'd been coming through New Appia twice a year for the previous seven, always stopped here at the hotel, and always come into the bar parlor to drink hot whisky with sugar water and chew my ear. He wore loud checked suits and fancy flannel waistcoats—I recollect the one on this night was tan, with orange nasturtiums embroidered on it—and he had muttonchop whiskers to go with his pointy mustache. He talked faster than most drummers, which is some fast, and told better dirty stories, too.

Now Tuggle sold all sorts of drugs and medicines—everything from hair tonic to laxatives, from Turkish Pile Ointment to Lydia Pinkham's Vegetable Compound for Ladies.

But what he sold best of all was a snake-oil product called Cherokee's Magical Herb Bitters. Likely most medicine drummers never touched a drop of what they peddled, but Tuggle swore up and down that he drank a full bottle of Cherokee's Magical Herb Bitters every week. I believed him, too, as passionate as he was on the subject. He was in the peak of health and says he owed it all to them bitters. Says it to anybody who'll listen. Says it to me every time he bellied up to my bar.

He come in after supper, this night I'm telling about. Carrying a tolerable load (which was nothing unusual), on account of he'd been imbibing spirits most of the day with his best customer, Chet Iams, over to the drugstore. He ordered a hot whisky with sugar water, made some small talk about the weather, and then commenced to bending my ear about them magical bitters of his. Not talking soft, neither. The other patrons sidled off, lest he include them in his pitch, but there wasn't nowhere for me to go. So I listened some as if I'd never heard it all before. Part of my job is to listen, even if it ain't always the best part.

Tuggle started out by saying that Cherokee's Magical Herb Bitters was just the tonic a man needed to stay fit in inclement weather like we was having, for it was the greatest blood and nerve medicine ever manufactured by human beings. Then he says: "Mister Fyfe, this miracle tonic cures all bilious derangements and drives out the foul corruption that contaminates the blood and causes decay. It stimulates and enlivens the vital functions, being as it is a pure vegetable compound and free from all mineral poisons. It promotes energy and strength, restores and preserves health, and infuses new life and vigor throughout the entire system." And so on and so forth.

He was just getting warmed up, old Tuggle was, when this young whippersnapper named Peckham come waltzing in.

Now Peckham was also a patent medicine drummer—a new-comer to our fair town, one of them freelancers that work for different manufacturers and don't have a set territory. Full of piss and vinegar, was young Peckham. Full of corn whisky, too, this night, on account of bending elbows all day long with a customer *he* was trying to impress. Weren't usual for two snake-oil peddlers to come through town at the same time, and this Peckham was new on the road, so him and Tuggle wasn't acquainted. Not yet, they wasn't.

Well, here come Peckham into the bar parlor, weaving some and toting his sample case, just as Tuggle declaims that Cherokee's Magical Herb Bitters is the purest, safest, and most effectual medicine known to mankind, and that there ain't no sore it won't heal, no pain it won't subdue, and no disease it won't cure.

Peckham stopped dead in his tracks, listening to this with a scowl. Then he twisted one of his sandy mustaches, and, when Tuggle paused to draw a breath, he says loud and clear: "Bunkum."

That got everybody's attention, including Tuggle's. Old Charley come around, looked the youngster up and down with one squinty eye, and asks him soft and chilly to repeat himself.

"Bunkum," Peckham says again, just as loud. "Pure bunkum."

"Is that so, my brash young fellow?" Tuggle says. "And just what do you know about such matters?"

"Everything I need to know," Peckham counters. "Why, whatever puny concoction you're hawking can't hold a candle to Doctor Wallmann's Celebrated Nerve and Brain Tonic."

"Doctor Wallmann's what?" Tuggle says, haughty. "I have never heard of it."

"You will," the boy says. "You surely will. It is brand spanking new . . . the finest, purest blood, nerve, and brain medicine ever made for the benefit of mankind. Bar none."

"Bunkum," Tuggle says.

Well, it got Sunday-sermon quiet in there. The two of 'em looked each other over like a couple of fancy fighting cocks. Then Peckham strutted up to the bar, opened his sample case, took out a brown bottle of this Dr. Wallmann's Celebrated Nerve and Brain Tonic, and smacked it down with a flourish. "Behold," he says. "The new wonder oil . . . the discovery of the ages."

Tuggle didn't even glance at the bottle. He reached inside his loud, checked coat, produced a brown bottle of Cherokee's Magical Herb Bitters, and smacked that down with an even grander flourish. "Behold," he says. "The old wonder oil . . . the *true* discovery of the ages."

The pair of 'em glared at each other. Then Peckham says by way of a challenge: "Doctor Wallmann's Celebrated Nerve and Brain Tonic cures any affliction you can name, and more afflictions and derangements than any other product on the face of the globe."

"Oh it does, does it?" Tuggle says. "Womb complaints and uterine affections, mayhap?"

"Of course."

"Formation of gas in the bowels?"

"Naturally."

"Sciatica and neuralgia?"

"Most assuredly."

"Chronic rheumatism, pleurisy, gout?"

"With ease, sir. With ease."

"Well, so does Cherokee's Magical Herb Bitters," Tuggle says like a senator to a rube, "and with even *greater* ease. My wonder bitters also cures dyspepsia, costiveness, bad breath, palpitations of the heart, the old Sunday sick headache, persistent and obstinate constipation, fever and ague, and salt rheum."

"So does my celebrated tonic," Peckham says. "Not to mention eczema, erysipelas, tetter, cankers, and water brash."

"But not ulcerated kidneys," Tuggle says.

"Ulcerated kidneys and inflamed kidneys."

"Highly colored urine?"

"*And* greasy froth in the urine."

"Asthma, bronchitis, epilepsy?"

"*And* purulent ulcers, scrofula, and deafness."

By this time Tuggle was red in the face—so red I couldn't help but wonder if Cherokee's Magical Herb Bitters also cured apoplexy. He all but shouts at the young upstart: "Belching of wind and food after eating?"

"With only two teaspoons."

"Lusterless eyeballs?"

"Three tablespoons."

"Catarrh of the bladder?"

"Half a bottle, no more."

"Lost manhood?"

"Guaranteed after the ingestion of but a single bottle."

"Liar!" Tuggle yells. "Charlatan! Only Cherokee's Magical Herb Bitters can stiffen a flaccid man's resolve!"

That got the boy's back up. He moved close to Tuggle and says right in his face: "How dare you call me a liar? I demand an apology, sir."

"To hell with your apology," Tuggle says. "And to hell with Doctor Pipsqueak's Celebrated Nerve and Brain Tonic!"

"Oh, yes?" Peckham says, sparking some himself. "Well, to hell with Quack's Magical damned Bitters!"

I leaned over the bar along in here and says—"Now, gents, settle down, let's keep matters peaceable."—but neither of 'em paid me any mind. They was nose to nose, glaring and growling.

"Diarrhea!"

"Lumbago!"

"Weak lungs!"

"Milk leg!"

"Chilblains and bunions!"

"Distressing heat flashes!"

"Diseased glands!"

"Carbuncles and cutaneous eruptions!"

"Dandruff and falling of the hair!"

"Pressure on top of the head!"

"I'll give you pressure on top of the head!" Tuggle roars, and danged if he don't fetch young Peckham a hellacious thump smack on the cranium.

Well, the blow knocked Peckham to his knees, but not for long. The youngster bounced back up like a jack-in-the-box, bellowing and snarling, and give old Charley a jolt over the heart. Next thing I knew, the two of 'em was mixing it up like a couple of crapulous prize fighters at the county fair—all flailing arms and patent-leather shoes and cuss words, some of which even I was amazed to hear.

By the time I got my bung starter and come over the bar, they was down on the floor, rolling around and punching, gouging and kicking each other. Everybody else had scattered out of harm's way. I leaned in and give Peckham a clout on the shoulder with the bung starter, on account of he'd picked up a spittoon and was aiming to brain Tuggle with it. Wasn't my best clout, though, for he did manage to land that spittoon alongside Tuggle's jaw with some weight behind it. Tuggle let out a bleat, and his eyes rolled up and out he went like a candle in a windstorm. Wasn't nothing I could do then but let Peckham have another whack with my bung starter, this one of the back of his noggin, which put *him* out cold, too, athwart Tuggle.

The other patrons crowded up, and we all looked down at them two sorry specimens. What a sight they was, lying there all bloody and bruised, fancy clothes in tatters, with not a lick of dignity left to either one. And all on account of some danged patent medicines that likely couldn't cure one in fifty of the ills and afflictions they was supposed to. Including and especially loss of manhood.

Harry Weems, the night clerk back then, was gawping in from the hotel lobby, and I hollered to him to run and fetch the sheriff. Then I went back around the bar for a swallow of something to settle my nerves. Not hardly Cherokee's Magical Herb Bitters and not hardly Dr. Wallmann's Celebrated Nerve and Brain Tonic. No sir—good old bourbon whisky.

Now, while we all waited for the sheriff, one of the regular customers picked up them two brown bottles that was setting side by side on the bar top and looked close at the labels. Then he let out a whoop and handed the bottles to me. And when I had a close look myself, what do you think I saw?

Why, both snake oils was manufactured by the John C. Delacroix Company of Chicago, Illinois. The same danged company! And neither of them peckerwoods had a clue until they woke up in jail together and the sheriff informed 'em.

Didn't I tell you old-time drummers was a caution?

Markers

Jack Bohannon and I had been best friends for close to a year, ever since he'd hired on at the Two Bar Cross, but if it hadn't been for a summer squall that came up while the two of us were riding fence, I'd never have found out who and what he was. Or about the markers.

We'd been out two weeks, working the range southeast of Eagle Mountain. The fences down along there were in middling fair shape, considering the winter we'd had. Bohannon and I sported calluses from the wire-cutters and stretchers, but, truth to tell, we hadn't been exactly overworking ourselves. Just kind of moving along at an easy pace. The weather had been fine—cool, crisp mornings, warm afternoons, sky scrubbed clean of clouds on most days—and it made you feel good just to be there in all that sweet-smelling open space.

As it happened, we were about two miles east of the Eagle Mountain line shack when the squall came up. Came up fast, too, along about three o'clock in the afternoon, the way a summer storm does sometimes in Wyoming Territory. We'd been planning to spend a night at the line shack anyway, to replenish our supplies, so as soon as the sky turned cloudy dark, we lit a shuck straight for it. The rain started before we were halfway there, and by the time we raised the shack, the downpour was such that you couldn't see a dozen rods in front of you. We were both soaked in spite of our slickers; rain like that has a way of slanting in under any slicker that was ever made.

The shack was just a one-room sod building with walls

coated in ashes-and-clay and a whipsawed wood floor. All that was in it was a pair of bunks, a table and two chairs, a larder, and a big stone fireplace. First things we did when we came inside, after sheltering the horses for the night in the lean-to out back, were to build a fire on the hearth and raid the larder. Then, while we dried off, we brewed up some coffee and cooked a pot of beans and salt pork. It was full dark by then, and that storm was kicking up a hell of a fuss; you could see lightning blazes outside the single window, and hear thunder grumbling in the distance and the wind moaning in the chimney flue.

When we finished supper, Bohannon pulled a chair over in front of the fire, and I sat on one of the bunks, and we took out the makings. Neither of us said much at first. We didn't have to talk to enjoy each other's company; we'd spent a fair lot of time together in the past year—working the ranch, fishing and hunting, a little mild carousing in Saddle River—and we had an easy kind of friendship. Bohannon had never spoken much about himself, his background, his people, but that was all right by me. Way I figured it, every man was entitled to as much privacy as he wanted.

But that storm made us both restless; it was the kind of night a man sooner or later feels like talking. And puts him in a mood to share confidences, too. Inside a half hour we were swapping stories, mostly about places we'd been and things we'd done and seen.

That was how we came to the subject of markers—grave markers, first off—with me the one who brought it up. I was telling about the time I'd spent a year prospecting for gold in the California Mother Lode, before I came back home to Wyoming Territory and turned to ranch work, and I recollected the grave I'd happened on one afternoon in a rocky meadow south of Sonora. A mound of rocks, it was, with a wooden marker anchored at the north end. And on the marker was an epitaph scratched out with a knife.

"I don't know who done it," I said, "or how come that grave was out where it was, but that marker sure did make me curious. Still does. What it said was . . . 'Last resting place of I. B. Lyon. Lived and died according to his name.' "

I'd told that story a time or two before, and it had always brought a chuckle, if not a horselaugh. But Bohannon didn't chuckle. Didn't say anything, either. He just sat looking into the fire, not moving, a quirly drifting smoke from one corner of his mouth. He appeared to be studying on something inside his head.

I said: "Well, *I* thought it was a mighty unusual marker, anyhow."

Bohannon still didn't say anything. Another ten seconds or so passed before he stirred—took a last drag off his quirly and tossed it into the fire.

"I saw an unusual marker myself once," he said then, quiet. His voice sounded different than I'd ever heard it.

"Where was that?"

"Nevada. Graveyard in Virginia City, about five years ago."

"What'd it say?"

"Said . . . 'Here lies Adam Bricker. Died of hunger in Virginia City, August, Eighteen Eighty-Two.' "

"Hell. How could a man die of hunger in a town?"

"That's what I wanted to know. So I asked around to find out."

"Did you?"

"I did," Bohannon said. "According to the local law, Adam Bricker'd been killed in a fight over a woman. Stabbed by the woman's husband, man named Greenbaugh. Supposed to've been self-defense."

"If Bricker was stabbed, how could he have died of hunger?"

"Greenbaugh put that marker on Bricker's grave. His idea of humor, I reckon. Hunger Bricker died of wasn't hunger for food, it was hunger for the woman. Or so Greenbaugh claimed."

"Wasn't it the truth?"

"Folks I talked to didn't think so," Bohannon said. "Story was, Bricker admired Greenbaugh's wife and courted her some. She and Greenbaugh weren't living together, and there was talk of a divorce. Nobody thought he trifled with her, though. That wasn't Bricker's way. Folks said the real reason Greenbaugh killed him was because of money Bricker owed him. Bricker's claim was that he'd been cheated out of it, so he refused to pay when Greenbaugh called in his marker. They had an argument, there was pushing and shoving, and, when Bricker drew a gun and tried to shoot him, Greenbaugh used his knife. That was his story, at least. Only witness just happened to be a friend of his."

"Who was this Greenbaugh?"

"Gambler," Bohannon said. "Fancy man. Word was he'd cheated other men at cards, and debauched a woman or two . . . that was why his wife left him . . . but nobody ever accused him to his face except Adam Bricker. Town left him pretty much alone."

"Sounds like a prize son-of-a-bitch," I said.

"He was."

"Men like that never get what's coming to them, seems like."

"This one did."

"You mean somebody cashed in his chips for him?"

"That's right," Bohannon said. "Me."

I leaned forward a little. He was looking into the fire, with his head cocked to one side, like he was listening for another rumble of thunder. It seemed too quiet in there, of a sudden, so I cleared my throat and smacked a hand against my thigh.

I said: "How'd it happen? He cheat you at cards?"

"He didn't have the chance."

"Then how . . . ?"

Bohannon was silent again. One of the burning logs slid off the grate and made a sharp, cracking sound; the noise seemed to jerk him into talking again. He said: "There was a vacant lot a few doors down from the saloon where he spent most of his time. I waited in there one night, late, and, when he came along, on his way to his room at one of the hotels, I stepped out and put my gun up to his head. And I shot him."

"My God," I said. "You mean you *murdered* him?"

"You could call it that."

"But damn it, man, why?"

"He owed me a debt. So I called in his marker."

"What debt?"

"Adam Bricker's life."

"I don't see. . . ."

"I didn't tell you how I happened to be in Virginia City. Or how I happened to visit the graveyard. The reason was Adam Bricker. Word reached me that he was dead, but not how it happened, and I went there to find out."

"Why? What was Bricker to you?"

"My brother," he said. "My real name is Jack Bricker."

I got up off the bunk and went to the table and turned the lamp up a little. Then I got out my sack of Bull Durham, commenced to build another smoke. Bohannon didn't look at me; he was still staring into the fire.

When I had my quirly lit, I said: "What'd you do after you shot Greenbaugh?"

"Got on my horse and rode out of there."

"You figure the law knows you did it?"

"Maybe. But the law doesn't worry me much."

"Then how come you changed your name? How come you traveled all the way up here from Nevada?"

"Greenbaugh had a brother, too," he said. "Just like Adam had me. He was living in Virginia City at the time, and he knows I shot Greenbaugh. I've heard more than once that he's looking for me . . . been looking ever since it happened."

"So he can shoot you like you shot his brother?"

"That's right. I owe him a debt, Harv, same as Greenbaugh owed me one. One of these days he's going to find me, and, when he does, he'll call in his marker, same as I did mine."

"Maybe he won't find you," I said. "Maybe he's stopped looking by this time."

"He hasn't stopped looking. He'll never stop looking. He's a hardcase like his brother was."

"That don't mean he'll ever cross your trail. . . ."

"No. But he will. It's just a matter of time."

"What makes you so all-fired sure?"

"A feeling I got," he said. "Had it ever since I heard he was after me."

"Guilt," I said, quiet.

"Maybe. I'm not a killer, not truly, and I've had some bad nights over Greenbaugh. But it's more than that. It's something I know is going to happen, like knowing the rain will stop tonight or tomorrow, and we'll have clear weather again. Maybe because there are too many markers involved, if you take my meaning . . . the grave kind and the debt kind. One of these days I'll be dead because I owe a marker."

Neither of us had anything more to say that night. Bohannon—I couldn't seem to think of him as Bricker—got up from in front of the fire and climbed into his bunk, and, when I finished my smoke, I did the same. What he'd told me kept rattling around inside my head. It was some while before I finally got to sleep.

I woke up right after dawn, like I always do—and there was Bohannon, with his saddlebags packed and his bedroll under one arm, halfway to the door. Beyond him, through the window, I could see pale gray light and enough of the sky to make out broken clouds; the storm had passed.

"What the hell, Bohannon?"

"Time for me to move on," he said.

"Just like that? Without notice to anybody?"

"I reckon it's best that way," he said. "A year in one place is long enough . . . maybe too long. I was fixing to leave anyway, after you and me finished riding fence. That's why I went ahead and told you about my brother and Greenbaugh and the markers. Wouldn't have if I'd been thinking on staying."

I swung my feet off the bunk and reached for my Levi's. "It don't make any difference to me," I said. "Knowing what you done, I mean."

"Sure it does, Harv. Hell, why lie to each other about it?"

"All right. But where'll you go?"

He shrugged. "Don't know. Somewhere. Best if you don't know, best if I don't know myself."

"Listen, Bohannon. . . ."

"Nothing to listen to." He came over and put out his hand, and I took it, and there was the kind of feeling inside me I'd had as a button when a friend died of the whooping cough. "Been good knowing you, Harv," he said. "I hope you don't come across a marker someday with my name on it." And he was gone before I finished buttoning up my pants.

From the window I watched him saddle his horse. I didn't go outside to say a final word to him—there wasn't anything more to say; he'd been right about that—and he didn't look back when he rode out. I never saw him again.

But that's not the whole story, not by any means.

Two years went by without me hearing anything at all about Bohannon. Then Curly Polk, who'd worked with the two of us on the Two Bar Cross and then gone down to Texas for a while, drifted back our way for the spring roundup, and he brought word that Bohannon was dead. Shot six weeks earlier, in the Pecos River town of Santa Rosa, New Mexico.

But it hadn't been anybody named Greenbaugh who pulled the trigger on him. It had been a local cowpuncher, liquored up, spoiling for trouble; and it had happened over a spilled drink that Bohannon had refused to pay for. The only reason Curly found out about it was that he happened to pass through Santa Rosa on the very day they hung the 'puncher for his crime.

It shook me some when Curly told about it. Not because Bohannon was dead—too much time had passed for that—but because of the circumstances of his death. He'd believed, and believed hard, that someday he'd pay for killing Greenbaugh. That there were too many markers in his life, and someday he'd die on account of one he owed. Well, he'd been wrong. And yet the strange thing, the pure crazy thing, was that he'd also been right.

The name of the 'puncher who'd shot him was Sam Marker.

"Give-A-Damn" Jones

The most admirable man I've ever known?

Gentlemen, that is a question that should require considerable thought and reflection. In my nearly seven decades of life I have traveled from one end of the country to the other, north and south of our borders and twice across the Atlantic Ocean. I have shaken hands with statesmen, been entertained by royalty, drunk brandy and smoked cigars with two sitting Presidents of these United States. I have known many celebrated and respected newspaper editors and publishers, among them my own father, the redoubtable William Satterlee. And I have spent hours in the company of famous authors, artists, philanthropists, and titans of commerce. The answer to your question should not roll easily off what one member of the fourth estate has seen fit to call "the golden tongue of Senator R. W. Satterlee." But the fact is, my answer requires not five seconds of brain cudgeling.

The most estimable and significant man of my acquaintance was a tramp printer named "Give-a-Damn" Jones.

No, no, I'm not pulling your legs. "Give-a-Damn" was the moniker bestowed upon him by his wandering brethren; his given name was Artemus. Artemus Jones. A tramp printer is what he was, in fact and in spirit, and proud of it.

Most of you are too young to recall the days when itinerant typesetters, a noble and misunderstood breed, were a vital element in the publishing of newspapers large and small. If you have read my resumé, you know that I myself was one of that adventurous fraternity in my early youth. Yet the tale of why I chose such a vagabond's trade is not nearly as well known as it should be. Nor, I dare say, is Artemus Jones and the rôle he played in the destiny of the man who stands before you. I have been remiss in publicly according him the credit he deserves. But no more, gentlemen. No more.

Make yourselves comfortable and I'll tell you why I place a traveling printer above any other man in my life.

It was the summer of 1883, two years after my father purchased the Bear Paw *Banner* and moved our family to that eastern Montana town from Salt Lake City. Bear Paw was generally a peaceful place, but in the spring of that year trouble had sprung up between nearby cattle ranchers and a group of German and Scandinavian farmers who had come west from Wisconsin and settled in the region. The farmers weren't squatters, mind you. The land they claimed was theirs free and clear. The cattlemen, however, had used it for beef graze for a generation and more, and considered the farmers an invasion force bent on using up precious water and destroying prime grassland. Feelings ran high on both sides, with most of Bear Paw siding with the Cattlemen's Association and its leader, Colonel Elijah Greathouse, owner of the sprawling Square G. Fistfights, fence-cutting, arson, two shooting scrapes, and one near lynching came of the disagreement, and there was as much name-calling and finger-pointing that spring and summer as you'll find on the floor of the United States Senate in session.

I was a mere lad of fifteen, but as interested as any full-grown adult in these volatile goings-on. My father, a man of strong opinions and iron will, had taken up the cause of the immigrant farmers and penned several fiery editorials defending their rights and denouncing the injustices perpetrated against them by their Bear Paw neighbors. As a result, the *Banner*'s plate-glass front window had been shattered by a rock one night, and the local job printer who had done our typesetting was intimidated by the cattlemen's interests into closing up shop and moving to Helena. William Satterlee had little choice but to set type himself, with my inexperienced help, except on those occasions when a tramp printer happened to stop off in our town.

In the three months before Artemus Jones arrived, an equal number of hand-peggers were hired. None lasted more than three days, and the only one who paid no attention to the uneasy climate was an old man of at least eighty years named Charlie Weems. He was completely toothless, though he chewed tobacco and could ring a spittoon at twenty yards with unerring accuracy; and he had but one eye, claiming to have lost the other in the explosion of a Queen Anne musket not long after the War of 1812. He drank forty-rod whisky from a seemingly bottomless flask, could recite the names and addresses of most houses of ill repute in the Western states and territories, cussed a blue streak while he worked, and set type faster than any man I have seen before or since. He boasted to me that he had never spent more than three days in any town, and he was true to his word where Bear Paw was concerned. There one day, gone the next, riding the rods or the blind baggage or tucked away in a boxcar on the Great Northern's east- or westbound night freight.

Another freight train, the tramp's favored form of transportation, brought Artemus Jones into our midst. I was alone in the *Banner* office when he walked in on a Tuesday morning. He was a lean, wiry man twice my age and a little more, with drooping, tobacco-stained mustaches and eyes a brighter blue than a Kansas cornflower. He wore a disreputable linen duster and carried a bindle wrapped in a bandanna handkerchief. Prepossessing? Not a bit. Yet despite an air of hard-bitten toughness, he was soft-spoken and polite and gave the impression of having more to him than met the eye. I sensed his profession even before he approached with the breed's standard opener: "How's work?" And after only a short while in his company, I sensed, too, that he was no ordinary man.

"Available," I said. "You'll be welcome. We go to press tomorrow night and circulate Thursday morning."

"Standard union wages?"

"Yes, sir. Twenty-five cents a thousand ems."

His blue eyes took my measure. "Young to be the owner of a territorial newspaper, aren't you?"

"William Satterlee is the owner. My father."

"William Satterlee, eh? I believe I've heard the name. And you'd be William, Junior?"

"No, sir. I go by R.W."

He barked a laugh. "You'll go places, then. Men with initials instead of given names always do. My name is Jones, Artemus Jones."

" 'Give-a-Damn' Jones?"

"So I've been called. How do you know the name?"

"We had a printer several weeks ago named Charlie Weems. He mentioned you."

"Toothless Charlie's still above ground, is he? I'm glad to hear it, even if he is an unrepentant old liar and sinner."

"He didn't say how you came by the moniker, Mister Jones."

"Nor will I." Short and sharp, as if he were embarrassed by the explanation. "I prefer to be called Artemus. Your father on the premises?"

"Off hunting news. He'll be back before long."

"Well, let's have a look at your shop while we wait."

I took him into the composing room and stood by while he

eyed our cranky old hand press, stone table, type frame, and cases. He opened upper- and lower-case drawers and nodded approvingly at the selection of Revier, nonpareil, and agate. Another approving nod followed his examination of the previous week's issue from a leftover bundle.

"This is tolerable good for a jim-crow sheet," he said— jim-crow being printer's slang for small-town. "Your father's been in the game a while, I take it."

"Two years in Bear Paw. Before that five years in Salt Lake, and before that stints in Sacramento and San Francisco, where I was born."

"I like working for a man who knows his business," Jones said. "Heard of the 'Perch of the Devil,' have you, R.W.?"

"Yes, sir!" I said. It was what Butte was called in those days. The copper mines there ran twenty-four hours, and the air was so poisonous thick with sulphur and arsenic fumes and smoke from roasting ores and smelter stacks that no vegetation was left anywhere in or near the town. This fact, plus its location on a steep hillside overlooking a bare butte, plus its reputation as the most wide-open camp in all of Montana had brought it the name. "Is that where you last worked?"

"It is."

"I've heard that on windless days, the smoke is so heavy over Butte it blots the sky and lamps have to be lit at midday."

"True, and then some."

"Which paper were you on? The *Miner* or the *Inter-Mountain*?"

"A. J. Davis's shop. Another man who knows his business."

I was impressed. A. J. Davis was editor and publisher of the *Inter-Mountain*, and reputed to be a stickler for hiring only the best among the typographers and reporters who applied. No "blacksmiths" for him!

"I was there a month," Jones said. "Wages cut above scale, but that wasn't the reason."

"No. What was?"

"Free beer on tap."

He went on to explain that above the *Inter-Mountain*'s offices was a saloon whose beer pipes happened to run through a corner of the composing room. One of the home-guard printers had devised a cleverly hidden plug for the pipe, all unknown to the saloonkeepers. Thus the printers had a constant supply of free suds whenever they felt thirsty.

Jones owned a storehouse of such anecdotes, and, when he was in a proper mood, he would regale me with one after another. He was also a fount of opinions, quotations, professional gossip, place descriptions, and capsule biographies of men and women he had known in his travels. He had been a roadster and gay cat, as young tramp printers were called in that era, since the age of fourteen and had crossed and recrossed the country half a dozen times. Yet he was reticent about his family background and personal life. He became rude and profane on the few occasions when I attempted to draw him out. And while it was plain that he shared his breed's liking for alcohol and ladies of easy virtue, he did no drinking on the job and was unfailingly courtly to women of every stripe.

He had worked for more than a few of the legends of newspapering, among them Joseph Pulitzer on the St. Louis *Post-Dispatch*, Edward Rosewater, the fighting editor of the Omaha *Bee*, and the beaver-hatted old firebrand, J. West Goodwin, of the Sedalia *Bazoo*. For a time he had traveled with "Hi-Ass" Hull, considered the king of the tramp printers for his union organizing work, whose nickname was derived from a Northwest Indian word meaning "tall man." For another period he'd run with the band of roaming typographers known as the Missouri River Pirates, who frequented the towns along the Missouri River between St. Louis and Sioux City. He had met Jesse James when the outlaw was living in St. Joseph under his Tom Howard alias, two days before the dirty little coward, Bob Ford, fired a .45 slug into Jesse's back. Others whose paths he'd crossed were Bat Masterson, Texas Jack Omahundro, the poet Walt Whitman, himself a tramp printer in New Orleans, and the acid-tongued San Francisco writer, Ambrose Bierce.

Artemus Jones had no formal education, but he was an erudite man. By his own estimate he had read two thousand books, the Bible more than once, and the entire works of Shakespeare. He could quote verbatim passages from the Book and the Bard two and three pages long. Poetry, too, everything from Lord Byron to bawdy limericks. And he conversed knowledgeably on politics, philosophy, art, music, what-have-you.

Now it may seem to you gentlemen that time has clouded my memory, led me to paint you a romanticized picture of this man Jones. You may even be thinking he was a blowhard, a dissembler, or both. I assure you, none of that is the case. My memory of Jones is as clear as spring water. He was exactly as I've described him, and within his province a wholly truthful and honorable man.

Well, then. My father put Jones to work, and an expert typographer he was. He handled planer, mallet, rule, and shooting stick as though he had been born with them in his hand, corrected misspellings without consulting a dictionary, plugged dutchmen in a pair of poorly spaced ads, and generally made the publication of that week's issue an easier task than usual. My father was pleased, and I confess I was in awe. I clung to Jones almost as tightly as his galluses, asking questions, begging more stories, listening with rapt attention to his every word.

William Satterlee's front-page editorial that week was particularly inflammatory—written, in Jones's considered opinion, with a pen dipped in snake venom. There had been another shooting shortly before Jones's arrival, of a farmer who had dared to stray onto Colonel Greathouse's land after a runaway horse. The horse had been shot dead and the settler severely wounded by two Square G fence riders. Sheriff Buckley ruled the shooting justifiable. My father damned Buckley, not for the first time, as an incompetent dullard in the moral, if not actual, pay of the Cattlemen's Association, and he demanded prosecution for murder not only of the two cowhands but of their employer, whom he called, among other things, a cowardly Napoléonic tyrant.

Now Elijah Greathouse was a proud man with a fearsome temper. He had been a brevet colonel with C Company of the Tenth Kansas Volunteers during the War Between the States, and, although he was rumored to have been roundly disliked as a bully by the soldiers under his command, he was boastful of his war record and his military background. The "cowardly Napoléonic tyrant" label infuriated him more than anything else my father had called him in print. The day after the issue appeared, he stormed into the *Banner* office with his foreman, a troublemaker and alleged gun artist named Kinch, and confronted William Satterlee.

"You retract that statement," he bellowed, "or by God you'll suffer the consequences."

My father was unruffled. "I don't respond to threats, Colonel."

"You'd damn' well better respond to this one. I mean what I say, editor. Write one more vicious lie about me and you'll pay dear, in one type of coin or another."

"You've made yourself clear. Before witnesses, I might add." Both Jones and I were standing in the composing room

117

doorway, where Greathouse and Kinch could plainly see us. Not that either of them seemed to take much notice. "Now I'll thank you and your cow nurse to get off my property."

Blood-rush turned Kinch's face the color of port wine. He stepped forward and poked my father in the chest with his forefinger. "Cow nurse, am I? Call me that again, you son-of-a-bitch, and you'll find out what else I am."

"I know what else you are," William Satterlee said meaningfully. "Get out before I summon that buffoon of a sheriff and have you arrested for harassment and public profanity."

The two cattlemen left, glaring and grumbling. Jones said to my father: "You've made bad enemies in those two, Mister Satterlee. I've seen their stripe before. Push them too far and one or both will act on their threats."

But my father was a stubborn man, and he had put blinders on where Greathouse and his foreman were concerned. "Humbug," he said. "Knaves, fools, and blowhards, the pair. I've nothing to fear from the likes of them."

Artemus Jones said no more. I held my tongue as well, though I was more than a little worried. No one had ever won an argument with my father when his back was up. Whenever I or anyone else tried, it served only to strengthen his conviction that he was in the right.

The next week passed swiftly. To my considerable pleasure, Jones stayed on in Bear Paw. He had built a stake, he said, working for A.J. Davis in Butte, and after the copper camp's rough and rowdy ways he was content to linger a while in calmer surroundings before moving on. He took a room at Ma Stinson's Travelers' Rest, a combination hotel and boarding house near the Great Northern dépôt that catered to railroad men, drummers, and transients. When he wasn't working, he spent most of his time at the Free and Easy Saloon, which had the best free lunch in Bear Paw. I suspect he also visited Tillie Johnson's parlor house, though I never dared to ask him.

In the composing room I watched his every move while he sat on the tall printer's stool, clad in his leather apron, and picked up the types and assembled them in the composing sticks. He showed great patience in answering the thousand and one questions I asked him about his trade and his travels. Prior to his coming, I had been uncertain of my future goals, though naturally I was tempted to follow my father's ink-stained profession. Before that week was out, I had decided unequivocally that an itinerant printer was what I wanted to be.

Jones neither encouraged nor discouraged me. His was a world of new vistas and high adventure, true, but it was also a lonely life, and a sometimes perilous one. I would have to be willing to take the bad with the good, he said, the hardships along with the ease and freedom of the open road. I allowed as how I could and would, and urged him to take me along when wanderlust claimed him again. He refused. Since his days with the Missouri River Pirates, he had traveled alone and preferred it that way. Besides, neither he nor anyone else could teach me the tricks of his trade—a man learned for himself and by himself. Some weren't cut out for the life and quit sooner or later for tamer, settled pursuits. Why, he had done some reporting here and there and been told by editors that he showed promise, and one day he might just take up that line himself. But when I pressed him, he admitted it was much more likely he'd remain an itinerant typographer until he was too old and infirm to ride the rails. Chances were, he said with a shrug, he would die in a strange town and be buried without a marker in a potter's field grave.

Well, this dissuaded me not at all. If anything, it strengthened my resolve to become a gay cat, to see and do the things and meet the people Jones had. By the end of the week I was making plans to leave Bear Paw on my sixteenth birthday. Plans that I may or may not have carried through, boyish as they were, if the events of that Saturday night had not taken place.

On Wednesday, fuel had been added to the strong feelings between cattlemen and farmers, in the form of a fire of dubious origin that claimed both the barn and house belonging to a homesteading family named Jansen. No one was seriously injured, though Jansen suffered burns in trying to save his livestock. It so happened the farmer's land bordered Colonel Greathouse's south pasture, and there had been a dispute between Jansen and Greathouse over water rights. My father took this to mean that the colonel was guilty of ordering the burnings. His front-page editorial was even more vitriolic than the previous week's, accusing the cattle baron outright and damning him as a savage oppressor who would commit any heinous crime to achieve his purposes.

I was helping Jones with the page lay-outs when William Satterlee came in with the editorial. Jones, while I peered over his shoulder, read it through in silence. Then he said: "Are you sure you want this to run as it stands, Mister Satterlee?"

My father was in an abrasive mood. "Don't ask foolish questions. And don't change so much as a comma when you set it."

"It's certain to provoke Colonel Greathouse."

"That doesn't concern me. What concerns me is his despicable behavior toward the settlers. If I don't take him to task for it, who will?"

"Father," I said, "suppose he does more this time than make idle threats? Suppose he comes after you?"

"He doesn't dare."

"Hadn't you better carry a side arm just in case? Or keep a shotgun by your desk?"

"You know how I feel about weapons and violence. I'll not be reduced to the tactics of men like Greathouse and Kinch, nor will I be intimidated by those tactics. I write the truth, and the truth is the only weapon I want or need." With these noble, if improvident, words, he stalked back into the office.

"Artemus," I said, "I think he's wrong, and I'm afraid for him. If he won't take up a side arm, maybe I should. . . ."

Jones fixed me with a sharp eye. "How much practice have you had with a handgun?"

"Not much, but I know how to shoot one."

"Graveyards are full of men who knew how to shoot guns, or thought they did. Lads your age, too."

"Do you own a pistol?" I asked.

"No."

"But don't you need one on the road, for protection?"

"Some think so. I'm not one of them. I've seen the results of too many gunfights. Your father's right to want to avoid violence if he can."

"But what if he can't? What if he has gone too far this time?"

"There's not much use," Jones said, "in crying fire before you see the flames."

I took his meaning well enough, but I didn't much care for it. I'd expected more of him than a tepid homily. That was all I was to get, however. Twice more I broached the subject that day, and both times he changed it, the last by launching into "The Girl with the Blue Velvet Band" in a rusty baritone. After that, I left him alone and fretted in private.

When the *Banner* appeared on Thursday, it caused the anticipated stir. Men and even a few women flowed in and out of the newspaper office, some to praise my father and more to berate him loudly. None of the visitors was Colonel Elijah

Greathouse, his foreman, or anyone else off the Square G. And what few threats were flung at William Satterlee were mild and seemed mostly wind.

Neither Greathouse nor any of his men showed on Friday, or on Saturday. My relief was tempered by the knowledge that the colonel could be a devious cuss. He might well be plotting a more subtle form of revenge, I thought, and I said as much to my father. He scoffed at the notion. William Satterlee was a brave and principled man, but his self-righteousness, his unshakable faith in his beliefs, at times made him his own worst enemy. In this case, as matters soon developed, it nearly cost him his life.

It was his custom to work late at the *Banner* most evenings, even on weekends. He would come home to take supper with my mother and me, then return to the office until eight or nine o'clock. Some evenings I joined him, but my mother did not care for my being out of a Saturday night. It was when cowhands rode in off the nearby ranches to let off steam, the saloons and parlor houses did a boisterous business, and now and then arguments were settled with pistols and knives. Farmers came to town then, too, and, with feelings running as high was they were, there were confrontations virtually every Saturday.

Time passed slowly, and, when my father had yet to come home by nine o'clock, I grew fearful enough to slip out through my bedroom window and hurry the few blocks to Main Street. From the hurdy-gurdy section near the railroad yards I could hear piano music and the shouts and laughter of revelers. But in the business district it was quiet, the street empty. Dark, as well, for the night was cloudy and moonless.

Lamplight shaped the *Banner*'s front window. Except for a flickery gas street lamp, it was the only light on the block. Or it was until I neared the building, passing by the alley that ran along its north side. Then, of a sudden, a different kind of light bloomed bright and smoky from the rear, and a faint crackling sound reached my ears.

Fire!

Heedlessly I plunged into the alley. It was our back wall that had been set ablaze, and, as I ran, Artemus Jones's words jolted into my mind: *There's not much use in crying fire until you see the flames.* I opened my mouth to cry it then, thinking to alert my father inside, but the shout was stillborn in my throat. For another cry sounded in that instant—the voice of William Satterlee, already alerted and coming through the rear door.

A scant few seconds later, as I ran clear of the alley, there was the *bang* of a pistol shot.

In the bright fire-glow I saw my father stagger and fall. I saw the other man clearly, too—Kinch, a smoking six-shooter in one hand and a tin of kerosene in the other. An anguished bellow burst from my throat. I stumbled and nearly fell myself. Kinch spun toward me, and, as I regained my balance, I saw his arm raise and his weapon level. I have no doubt he would have shot me dead within another two or three heartbeats. His face was twisted unnaturally, his eyes wild in the firelight.

It was Artemus Jones who saved my life.

He came lunging through the door, his arm upraised, a short, blunt object jutting from his closed fist, and shouted—"Kinch! Not the boy, Kinch, *me!*"—in a thunderous voice. No man could have ignored the savage menace in that cry. Kinch swung away from me as Jones charged him. The pistol banged again. Jones's left arm jerked, but the bullet's impact neither stopped nor slowed his rush. He flailed downward with what was clutched in his right hand—a printer's mallet, I realized in the instant before it connected with Kinch's head. The sound of wood colliding with flesh and bone was audible even above the crackling of the flames. The Square G foreman went down all of a piece, with no buckling of his legs—dead before his body settled into the grass.

Jones dropped the mallet and knelt beside my father. "He's still alive!" he called as I started toward him. "Run and fetch a doctor, R.W. Quick!"

I turned and ran. Other men were drawing near on Main Street, summoned by the gunshots. I was aware of lantern light and raised voices as I raced upstreet to Dr. Ferris's house. It took what seemed eons to rouse him from his bed and into his clothes, lead him back to the newspaper building. The flames had been mostly extinguished by then, a dozen men having formed a bucket brigade and others wielding burlap sacks from the feed and grain store. So intent was I on my father's motionless body, it was not until the next day that I learned the fire damage had been confined to a charred wall and portion of the roof.

Jones was again on one knee beside him, his left arm loose and dripping blood. In spite of his wound he had brought out a cushion to prop up William Satterlee's head and a blanket to cover him. The bullet had entered my father's chest, but its path had missed any vital organs. When I heard Dr. Ferris say—"I don't believe it's a mortal wound."—my limbs went jellied with relief.

The rest of that night is a blur in my memory. I recall a long vigil with my mother at the doctor's house, and at some point a brief conversation with Artemus Jones. The damage to his arm was minor, requiring no more than an application of carbolic salve and a bandage. He had no difficulty in using it.

When I thanked him, belatedly, for saving my life, he said in gruff tones: "You shouldn't have been there. And there shouldn't have been any gun play."

". . . What do you mean?"

"Your father was on his way to the privy when he heard Kinch outside . . . he was already through the door before I could react. Else I'd have been the first one out."

"Then you'd have been shot instead."

"Maybe not. I can throw a mallet as well as swing one."

It took a short while for the significance of this to sink in. "You had no reason to be at the office so late tonight," I said then, "unless you were as worried as I was. On guard even if my father wasn't."

Jones shrugged and made no reply.

"But why?" I asked. "It wasn't your trouble."

"I had my reasons."

"You might have been killed. . . ."

"I might have," he said, "but I wasn't. Some chores are worth doing, R.W., for your own sake as well as others'."

I understood that, and something else then, too. I understood why he was called "Give-a-Damn" Jones.

As serious as William Satterlee's wound was, he was conscious and out of danger by sunup. My mother and I went to church to give thanks, and, when we returned to the doctor's, we found a surprise visitor—Colonel Elijah Greathouse. News of the shooting, attempted arson, and Kinch's demise had been delivered to him by another of his cowhands, and he had come to town, he said stiffly, for only one reason. To tell Sheriff Buckley and now my father that Kinch had acted on his own, in this case and in the burning of the Jansen homestead. Despite William Satterlee's public opinion, he neither ordered nor sanctioned senseless violence. Greathouse swore to this with his hand on a Bible he produced from his coat pocket. Afterward, he turned on his heel and walked out.

Admitting to mistakes in judgment was never easy for my father, but no man lying flat on his back with a punctured chest can be as cocksure as when healthy and standing tall. He offered a brief, grudging apology to Jones and me, and, when the sheriff came to see him, he made no attempt to bring charges against Colonel Greathouse. Later, after his recovery, he softened his editorial stance considerably. Still later, when a harsh winter forced an uneasy alliance between ranchers and farmers, he ceased taking sides altogether. There were no more clashes between him and the colonel. They never spoke to each other again.

Artemus Jones did not leave Bear Paw immediately, as I'd been afraid he would. He stayed for three more weeks, while my father slowly mended. To everyone's surprise, Jones volunteered to act as both the *Banner*'s editor and typesetter during the convalescence. I was delighted when William Satterlee, a newspaperman above all else, agreed. He seemed to take it for granted that Jones was monentarily motivated, but I knew better.

Jones and I worked tirelessly during those three weeks. In addition to his other duties he wrote most of the news copy and a pair of editorials on brotherhood and Christian charity. If his style was rough-edged, it was also sincere, forthright, and offensive to no one. And for good measure, he made sure that in none of the issues he edited was there a single typographical or grammatical error, unplugged dutchman, pied line, or widow.

By the middle of the third week my father was well enough to return to his desk and pen that week's editorial, in which his praise of Jones was, for him, lavish. Upon reading it, Artemus refused to do the setting and argued in vain against its publication. William Satterlee won the argument, as he always did when hale and hearty, but it was I who set the type. My father also paid Jones, in addition to his printer's wages, a bonus of twenty-five dollars for his editorial work. Jones took the money with no particular reluctance and, in the tramp's typically profligate fashion, spent most, if not all, of it over the next two days at the Free and Easy and Tillie Johnson's.

The day after that, Saturday, he packed his bindle and hopped one of the Great Northern's night freights for parts unknown.

He said nothing to my father or me about moving on. He was not a man for good byes, any more than a man for praise or conceit or sentiment. There one day, gone the next. True to himself, his calling, and his principles in every way.

Well, gentlemen, there you have it, in sum and without embellishment. Why Artemus Jones is the most admirable man I have ever known.

Did we meet again? To my everlasting regret, we did not. I left Bear Paw myself shortly after my sixteenth birthday, and for the next six years I followed the adventurous trail of the itinerant printer across the width and breadth of the country. I encountered men who knew Jones and spoke highly of him, and twice I arrived in cities—Joplin, Missouri, and Spokane, Washington—a few short days after he'd been there and traveled on. But not once, despite my best efforts, did our roaming paths cross.

As many of you know, I left the wanderer's life in 1890, to take the position of police reporter on the Baltimore *Sun*. Newspapering was as much in my blood as printer's ink, but that was not the only reason I settled down. The day of the tramp typographer was drawing to a close. The mechanical age was upon us, and a new-fangled machine in which matrices ran down channels and were assembled to cast a whole line of type at one time—the Linotype, of course—had come into widespread use. Some of the old hand-peggers reluctantly learned the new device and became home-guards in various cities and towns. Others threw out their stick and rule, gave up their union cards, and took the same route as I or embarked on different careers entirely. Only a few hung on to the very end of their days taking catch-as-catch-can type-setting jobs, living hand-to-mouth on the open road.

It is my belief that Artemus Jones was among that last, ever-dwindling group. If he is still above ground, he is an old man, as old as toothless Weems and doubtless as feisty, and still hand-pegging in some backwater shop. More likely he has gone on to his reward, having fulfilled his own prophecy of death in a strange town and burial in an unmarked potter's field grave.

Were it ever in my power to determine his final resting place, I would erect upon it a marble stone engraved with his name and the words: "He gave a damn about his fellowman." That was the credo he lived by, gentlemen—and it is the credo I adopted for myself. Where I have succeeded in following it, the credit is largely his. And where I have failed, the failings are R. W. Satterlee's alone.

The Gambler

For most of his life, he said, nigh on fifty years, he'd been a sporting man. Faro, that was his game, he said. He'd operated faro banks all over the West, been a mechanic in some of the fanciest gambling houses from one end of the frontier to the other. Poker? Sure, that too. He'd played poker and Brag for big stakes. Three-card monte and twenty-one and Pitch and just about any other card game you could name. His hands weren't much to look at now, all crippled up with arthritis like they were, but once, why, he could hold one deck in the palm of his hand while he shuffled up another. That wasn't the least of what he could do, neither. He'd always been a square gambler . . . well, almost always, fella sometimes hit a losing streak and he had to eat then too, didn't he? Not that he'd ever worked any big-time gyps or cons, mind. Just every now and then held out an ace or stacked a deck whilst shuffling or reversed a cut—and done it in the company of men like Dick Clark and Frank Tarbeaux and Luke Short and the Earp brothers, with them watching with their hawk's eyes and never suspecting a thing. That was how good a mechanic *he* was in his prime.

Those had been wild times, he said, desperate times. But from soda to back, they'd also been grand times. Oh, Lordy, what grand times they had been!

Thing was, he hadn't set out to enter the Life. No, when he'd left Ohio for California that summer of '54, it had been gold mining that was on his mind. Just sixteen that summer, all fixed to help work his brother John's claim in the Mother Lode. But when he got to Columbia, the gem of the southern mines, he'd found poor John a month dead of consumption and his claim sold off to pay debts—and *him* with just two dollars left out of his traveling money. Only job he could get was swamping at the Long Tom.

Hardly a man left now that remembers the Long Tom, he said, but in its day it was the swellest gambling house in Columbia, and Columbia itself the rip-snortin'est town in the whole of the Mother Lode. Thirty saloons, a stadium for bull and bear fights, close to a hundred and fifty faro banks . . . why, there hasn't been a town like it since, except maybe Tombstone in the 'Eighties. And that Long Tom, well, that Long Tom was so big it ran from one street clean through to another, with a doorway at either end. Twenty-four tables, twelve on each side of a center aisle wide as a stagecoach runway. Guards on both doors, two armed floormen, and, when there was a ruckus, those guards would draw their pistols and shoot out the big whale-oil lamps that hung over the aisle, and then the doormen would lock the doors, and the floormen would shine dark lanterns on the gents that were cheating or otherwise causing trouble and put an end to it, peaceable or unpeaceable. Then the floormen would rig up new lights, and the games would commence again just as though nothing had happened.

Well, the Long Tom was owned by the Mitchell brothers, and what they did was they rented out those twenty-four tables to professional gamblers like Charles Cora, who later on got himself hung for murder by the vigilantes in San Francisco, and Ad Pence and Governor Hobbs and John Milton Strain. Now John Milton Strain was a gold-hunter as well as a gambler, and he didn't mind taking a young buck along with him to do some of the hard labor. Also didn't mind teaching a young buck the ins and outs of the sporting trade. So that was how he'd learned cards, he said—from John Milton Strain, one of the best of the old-time cardsharps. (Wasn't any slouch when it came to prospecting, neither, was John Milton. One day he found a gold nugget as big as an adobe brick, ten inches wide and five inches thick—all high-grade ore that he melted down into a bar weighing more than thirty pounds. Sleeper's Gold Exchange paid him $7,500 for that bar. $7,500 for one bar of pure gold!)

He'd worked at the Long Tom three years, he said, learning the gambling trade from John Milton Strain . . . well enough finally so that he'd rented his own faro lay-out right alongside John Milton's. He might have stayed on longer, except that a fire burned the Long Tom down in '57—burned twelve square blocks of Columbia's business district along with it. The Mitchell brothers put up a new building, but John Milton had had his fill of Columbia by then, and he decided he'd had his, too. So the two of 'em set out together for greener pastures.

He'd spent nearly ten years touring the mining camps in California and Nevada, about half that time with John Milton Strain for a partner. During those years he learned to hold his own with just about anybody in a "hard cards" game for big stakes. Won more than he lost, consistent, and if it hadn't been for a fondness for hard spirits and the company of fast women, why he'd have been a rich man before he was thirty. Yes, sir, a rich man. But money was made to be spent, that was his philosophy. The more he made, the hotter it got sitting there in his pockets, and, when it commenced to burn holes, well, what was there to do then but take it out and spend it?

By early '66 he'd had enough of the mining camps; he craved a look at other parts of the frontier, a chance to play with the bigger names in the sporting trade. So he'd drifted east and north, he said, up to Montana and then down to

Cheyenne, Wyoming, which was a wide-open town in those days. Plenty of sports there, all right, most of them with the Hell-on-Wheels crowd that was following the construction of the Union Pacific Railroad west from Omaha to Promontory Point, Utah.

Now along that Union Pacific route, he said, the railroad set up supply points and campgrounds for track workers and other laborers—impermanent tent-towns for thousands of men. Well, those railroaders played as hard as they worked, so it was only natural that the honky-tonkers would gravitate to the camps to oblige them. In Cheyenne, one of the few real towns along the route, he'd found scores of gamblers, square and sure-thing both, and dozens of small-timers working as ropers, cappers, and steerers. Madams and whores and pimps, too. And saloon operators and confidence men and dips and yeggs—the whole shebang. And what they'd do, every time the railroad moved its base of operations a little farther west, was to pack up *their* equipment and move right along with 'em. That was how the whole business came to be called Hell-on-Wheels.

He'd joined up with 'em in Cheyenne and stayed on through Fort Saunders and Laramie and Benton City. Crazy wild, those days were, he said. He'd teamed with Ornery Ed Meeker on a brace faro game, and in Fort Saunders he found out Meeker was holding out on him and they'd had it out, and one Sunday afternoon he'd shot Meeker dead. Yes, sir, one clean shot right in his whiskers. First man he'd ever killed, but not the last. Then he fell in with one of Eleanore Dumont's working girls, to his sorrow, for she stole three thousand dollars he'd won at faro and decamped with the money and a fellow named Peavey, one of Corn-Hole Johnny Gallagher's steerers.

Well, it was just crazy wild. And the wildest place of all was

Benton City, which they came into the summer of '68. Hot? Lordy, it was hot that summer! North Platte River was two miles away, and the water-haulers charged a dollar a barrel and ten cents a bucket; they had the best graft in town, by a damn' sight. He'd worked the Empire Tent there, on account of it was the biggest operation and got the heaviest play, and he figured he could make more than he could with his own box. Fellow who ran the Buffalo Hump Corral wanted him in there, too—offered him a piece of the action—but the Buffalo Hump specialized in a game called rondo coolo, which you played with a stick and ivory balls on a billiard table, and what did he know about a game like that? He was a card man, a faro dealer and poker sharp. That was what he knew and that was how he made his living.

He was working the Empire Tent when *he* got shot. Railroad worker accused him of marking cards, which he hadn't been, and hauled out a Colt six-gun and put a slug in his left arm before he could bring his own weapon to bear. Well, he almost died. Almost lost his left arm and almost died, but if he *had* lost that arm he'd have wished he *had* died, he said, because how could a one-armed gambler expect to make out?

Took him three months to recover, and by then the Hell-on-Wheels bunch was getting ready to move on to the next stop. They left a hundred dead behind them, their own and railroaders both—a hundred in three months. And him with that busted wing and most of his cash gone for doctoring and what-not. So he'd called it quits, right then and there. Hell-on-Wheels wasn't for him. Killed a man and almost been killed himself . . . no, sir, that wasn't for him any more.

So he'd commenced to drifting again, building up stakes and losing 'em and building 'em back up again. Out to Kansas for a spell, Dodge City and the other cow towns. Shot a man in the Long Branch in Dodge one day, but the fellow didn't die; wasn't his fault that time neither, he said. Then, in '73, he'd got wind of a big silver strike in California, down in the Panamint Mountains, and of a new camp that had sprung up there called Panamint City.

Town was wide open when he got there, he said. They called it "a suburb of hell," which he didn't think it was so far as sin was concerned, not after Hell-on-Wheels—but, Lordy, it was *hot* as hell, up there above the floor of Death Valley like it was. Made the Wyoming plain seem like a cool riverside retreat.

First thing, he'd gone to work as a mechanic for Jim Bruce at the Dempsey and Boultinghouse Saloon. Now Bruce was a hardcase, having ridden the Missouri-Kansas border with Quantrill, and he didn't take kindly to insults and trouble-makers. Another dealer, name of Bob McKenny, ran afoul of Bruce and tried to kill him, and what happened was, Jim Bruce blew his fool head off. And what did he do then, straightaway? Why, he took Bob McKenny right out and buried him, that's what he did, on account of Jim Bruce wasn't just a gambler, he was also Panamint City's undertaker!

Well, he said, after a year or so he started dealing for Dave Neagle at Dave's resort, the Oriental, which had a fancy black walnut bar and some of the spiciest paintings of the female form divine that a man ever set eyes on. He stayed on there for four years, and would have stayed longer, likely, for he and Dave Neagle got on fine, and he'd taken up with one of the girls at Martha Camp's bawdy house, Sadie her name was, blonde and plump like the women in the paintings over the Oriental's black walnut bar. But then a big rainstorm hit the Panamints, and a flash flood came boiling down from the heights and swept up more than a hundred buildings as if they were bunches of sticks, the Oriental among 'em, and washed the wreckage all the way down Surprise Cañon and spread it over a mile of Panamint Valley. Hadn't been for somebody up at one of the stamp mills spotting the flood and raising an alarm, he said, him and most of the other townspeople would have gone sailing down Surprise Cañon, too.

From there he'd gone up to Bodie for a while, and then on back to Kansas and the queen of the cow towns. But Dodge wasn't what she had been a decade earlier, he said, leastways not so far as a sporting man was concerned, and he hadn't stayed long—just long enough to get wind that Dick Clark and Lou Rickabaugh and Bill Harris, who had once owned the Long Branch, had gone into partnership and opened a resort out in Tombstone. Well, he'd never met Dick Clark and wished he had, for Clark was a legend among sporting men, so he'd set out for Arizona Territory. And when he arrived in Tombstone, why Dick Clark was every bit the gentleman he was reputed to be, and his Oriental Saloon and Gambling Hall at Allen and Fifth streets was by far the grandest gambling house in town. Fancy chandeliers and colored crystals set into the bar, which was finished in white and gilt, and a club room to knock the eye out of a Victorian swell . . . oh, it was grand! He'd never been in a grander place before nor since, he said.

Now Dick Clark, as befitted his station, had some mighty important gents dealing for him. He had Luke Short and Bat Masterson and Wyatt Earp and Doc Holliday, among others, and he paid them twenty-five dollars for a six-hour shift— princely wages for those times. That was where he wanted to work, no question about that, so he'd talked to Dick Clark and danged if Dick Clark hadn't hired him. And there he was, he said, dealing at the Oriental Saloon with Luke Short and Wyatt Earp and Doc Holliday and Bat Masterson, all of them swell fellows and don't let anybody tell you different.

Bat Masterson didn't stay long, having fish to fry elsewhere, but Wyatt and Doc, they stayed, and everybody knows what happened with them. Well, sure—they and Wyatt's brothers, Virgil and Morgan, got into a feud with the Clantons and the McLaury brothers and Curly Bill Brocius and John Ringo, and it all came to a head late in '81 when Morgan Earp got himself ambushed, and then Wyatt went out in a vengeful rage and done for Curly Bill and a couple of others in the Clanton crowd. That was when they had the big shoot-out at the O.K. Corral. He was there that day, and he'd seen it all, he said. He'd seen the whole thing from soda to hock.

Nor was that all he'd seen that year, he said. He'd seen Luke Short gun down Charlie Storms, a hardcase who'd been one of the Hell-on-Wheels bunch. Happened right there in the Oriental, right smack in front of *his* table. It was Charlie Storms's doing, he said, no question about that, for he was a mean one and had been in several gunfights in Cheyenne and Deadwood and Leadville, and wanted to add an important name to his list of victims. But he met his match in Luke Short. He goaded little Luke, and goaded him some more, and then, when push came to shove, why Luke outdrew him cool as you please, and Charlie Storms died a surprised man.

Tombstone in the 'Eighties was a fine place to be, he said, and he'd felt settled there, working for Dick Clark. Now and then he'd develop an itch, same as Dick Clark himself would, and get on a stagecoach and see what Lady Luck had in store in places like Tucson and Phoenix and Prescott and Las Vegas, New Mexico. But he never stayed long in any of those places—particularly not in Las Vegas, where he himself had been goaded into killing his second and last man, this time in a misunderstanding over a woman. He always went back to Tombstone and the Oriental Saloon and Gambling Hall. He was still dealing there, he said, when Dick Clark sold out his interest in '94 and retired from the Life.

He was likewise of retirement age by then, but unlike Dick

Clark and some of the other old-timers who'd made their for-
tunes and bought houses and saloons and other property, or
invested their money in stocks and bonds and such and were
comfortably fixed for the rest of their days, *he* was still just a
mechanic. Flush some of the time, broke more often. Never
saved any of his winnings, never invested any of it, or bought
any property other than what he could carry in a pair of car-
petbags. Sport like him couldn't afford to retire. All he could
do, he said, was keep right on dealing cards.

So after Dick Clark sold out his interest in the Oriental,
he'd gone on down to Bisbee, which was still a fair hot town
in the mid-'Nineties, and worked for a time in Cobweb Hall.
Then he'd moved on to Phoenix and Prescott, and then up to
Virginia City, Nevada, and then over to Albuquerque. He
was in Albuquerque when the new century came in, he said,
sixty-two years old and stony broke in New Mexico. But then
he'd won a stake and moved on to Taos, and then over into
Texas—San Antonio and El Paso and Austin and Tascosa—
and then back into Arizona Territory, to see if Tombstone
was anything like it had been in the old days. But it wasn't.
No sir, *none* of the towns was like they'd been in the old days.
They were all changed, and still changing so fast you could
almost see it happening right before your eyes.

Once, he said, the sporting man had commanded respect.
Not just the high-rollers like Dick Clark, no, ordinary sports
like himself. Why, you could walk down the street in just
about any town and gents would doff their hats and smile and
wish you good day. Women would smile, too, some of them,
and more than you'd think would do more than smile. Oh,
you were somebody in those days, he said. You had a skill few
had, and you made big money, and you were somebody and
you had respect.

But not after the new century came in. Not after all the

people moved west and shrank the land and tamed it. Everything changed then. Men quit smiling and doffing their hats and wishing you good day. Woman wouldn't have anything to do with you, none except the whores. They all whispered behind your back and gave you dirty looks and shunned you like you were a common thief. And then the territorial leaders that wanted statehood, they went and put those laws in, all those anti-gambling laws. Blamed gambling and sporting men for society's ills and took away their livelihood and made them outlaws and outcasts.

It wasn't fair, he said, it wasn't right. What could men like him do, men who'd been in the Life for nigh on fifty years? Where could they go? Some took to running illegal games, sure, but those were the young ones. What about the ones past their prime, old men with hands starting to cripple with arthritis? What about them?

Memories, that was all they left him. Fifty years of memories . . . all the places he'd been, all the things he'd seen and done, all the men and women he'd known. He'd seen it all in those fifty years, by grab. He'd *lived* it all. Been a part of the wildness, and of the slow taming, too. But now . . . now the land was too tame, it was like a tiger that had become a pussycat. This wasn't the frontier any more, a place with growl and howl; this was just a tamed tiger meowing in the sun.

Well, he remembered the old days, he said. *He* knew how wild and desperate those times had been. And how grand, too. Oh, Lordy, what grand times they had been!

They found him one morning in the dust behind Simpson's Barber Shop, lying crumpled in the dust with his nightshirt pulled up to expose the swollen veins in his pipe-stem legs. He must have come out during the night to use the outhouse, the town marshal said. Left his room at the rear of the shop, where Simpson had let him live in exchange for sweeping up, and set out for the privy and had a seizure before he got there. He hadn't died right away, though. He'd crawled a ways, ten feet or so toward the privy; the marks were plain in the dust.

That afternoon, the undertaker and his assistant put the corpse in a plain pine box, loaded the box into the mortuary wagon, and drove up the hill to the cemetery. The only other citizen to go along with them was the preacher, but he didn't tarry long. The old man hadn't been religious and had never attended church services; it was only out of common decency that the preacher had decided to speak a few words over the grave. Besides, it was hot that day. Hot as the hinges of hell, the preacher said, just before he rode his horse back down the hill.

The undertaker and his assistant made short work of the burying and laid their tools in the wagon. The assistant mopped his sweating face with his handkerchief, spoke then for the first time since their arrival.

"You think he *was* a sporting man?"

"That old coot?" the undertaker said. "Now what makes you ask that?"

"Well, all those stories he would tell. . . ."

"Stories, that's all they were. Old man's imaginings. He had nothing when he come here and nothing when he died. No money, no kin, no friends to speak of . . . nobody, even, to buy him a marker for his final resting place. And him supposed to have been a fancy cardsharp rubbing elbows with Wyatt Earp and Bat Masterson? Pshaw!"

The undertaker shook his head, turned to look down the dry brown hill at the dry brown town crouching in the summer heat, at the desert beyond, rolling away like a dead sea toward the horizon.

"Wasn't nobody at all," he said.

139

Wooden Indian

I was laying a fire in the cast-iron stove when Henry Bandelier, who owns the Elk Basin General Merchandise Store, came rushing into my office. Usually Bandelier is the unflappable sort, but he was in a dither this cold October morning; he was so flappable, in fact, with his feet moving and his arms sawing up and down, he looked like a scrawny pink crow about to take flight.

"Sheriff, I been robbed!"

That brought me right up to attention. I didn't much care for Bandelier—he was a loudmouth, and no more honest than he had to be—but you don't have to care for a man to do your duty by him.

"The hell you say. When did it happen?"

"Middle of the night," he said.

"How much is missing?"

"How much? *All* of it, of course!"

"All the money in your cashbox?"

"Money? Who said anything about money?"

"Well, you did . . . didn't you?"

"No! Wasn't money that was stolen. It was my Indian."

"Come again?"

"You heard me, Sheriff. My prize wooden Indian's been pilfered."

"Now who in the world would steal that monstros . . . ?" I stopped, cleared my throat, and started over. "That Indian's been setting out in front of your store six or seven years now. Weighs two hundred pounds if it weighs an

140

ounce. Who'd want to go and steal it?"

"Tom Black Wolf, that's who."

"Oh, now. . . ."

"It's a fact," Bandelier said. "You can't go sticking up for that boy this time, Lucas Monk. Him and that cousin of his, Charlie Walks Far, stole my Indian in the dead of night, and that's the plain truth."

"How do you know it was them?"

"Lloyd Cooper told me so, that's how I know. He was awake at three a.m., using his chamber pot, and he heard a wagon rattling by the hotel and looked out, and it was Tom Black Wolf and Charlie Walks Far making off with my Indian."

"How could Lloyd tell who was on the wagon, at that distance?"

"There was a moon last night," Bandelier said. "You know that as well as I do. A big fat harvest moon. Lloyd saw them plain. Saw something eight feet long in the bed, too, under a piece of canvas. Said it looked like a body. Ain't anything eight feet long that looks like a covered-up corpse, by God, except my Indian."

That was open to debate, but trying to argue with a fractious Henry Bandelier was like trying to argue with a mean-spirited bull in rutting season. I said: "All right, Mister Bandelier. You just simmer down. I'll drive out to the reservation and have a talk with Tom Black Wolf."

"Talk with him, hell. You arrest him, Sheriff, you hear me? You arrest him and bring back my Indian, or I'll know the reason why!" He turned on his heel and stalked out.

I stood puzzling for a time in the cold office. *The reason why.* Well, that was the question uppermost in my mind, even if it wasn't uppermost in Henry Bandelier's. What would a couple of Indians want with an eight-foot, two-hundred pound wooden Indian?

★ ★ ★ ★ ★

The damned Model T wouldn't start without I spent twenty minutes at the crank, aggravating my bursitis with every turn. Contraption never failed to give me trouble as soon as the weather turned frosty. Come the winter snows, I'd lock it in my barn again and leave it there until the thaw. Progress is all well and good, and in 1915 a county sheriff's got to have a modern conveyance, or folks don't think he's serious about his job, but if you ask me, a good horse is a better asset to a man than any motorcar ever manufactured. Horses don't freeze up in the winter, for one thing. And you don't have to crank one until your arm pretty near falls off to get it started on cold mornings.

I pedaled the flivver into low gear and drove on down Main Street, with the exhaust farting smoke and sparks all the way. The front of Henry Bandelier's store looked some better without that wooden Indian rearing up next to the entrance. Most folks in Elk Basin would agree with that, too. Bandelier had had more than one complaint about it over the years. But he was right paternal about that Indian, which was ironical because he didn't like real Indians at all. He'd trade with the ones on the reservation, but he made them come around to the rear so as not to *offend* his white customers. He claimed the wooden Indian had been a gift from the Cuba Libre Cigar Company of Cleveland, Ohio, in honor of the fact that he sold more Cuba Libre crooks and panatelas than any other merchant in the state. More likely, he'd made some kind of deal with the Cuba Libre people to display that Indian, which had their name written across the chest in bold red letters, in exchange for a fatter discount. Either way, it was an eyesore. And not just on account of its size. It was rough-carved of some tobacco-spit brown wood, the limbs and head were all out of proportion to the body, a piece of the nose had been shot off by a drunken cowboy one Fourth of July, and the cigars it was clutching were so big and phallic-looking they'd caused more than one woman to blush when Bandelier first unveiled it.

Officially, though, that wooden Indian might have been the Mona Lisa: it was stolen property, its theft a felony offense. The law's the law, and I'm sworn to uphold it. But it sure would pain me to have to arrest Tom Black Wolf and Charlie Walks Far for the crime. Especially young Tom.

He was twenty-two, smart as a whip, and down-deep honest. You could trust him with your money and likely your life, which is a hell of a lot more than I'd say for most white men in Elk Basin. He'd whizzed through agency school, and at the urging of Abe Fetters, the Indian agent, and Doc Cranston and me and a couple of others, he'd come in to attend high school right here in town. Graduated at the top of his class, too. He wanted to be an agronomist. I had to go look that up. It means somebody who specializes in field-crop production and soil management, which is to say somebody who can make crops grow on poor land. He'd applied to the state university and been accepted and would have enrolled last semester—he'd been working two jobs off the reservation to save up enough for his tuition—except for his grandfather, old Chief Victor who had once been a great warrior and who was descended from and named after the head chief of the Flatheads during the middle of the last century. He just wouldn't leave the reservation while the old man was on his deathbed. Well, Chief Victor had been on his deathbed three months now and was likely to lie there another three before he finally let go. These old warriors die hard.

So that was Tom Black Wolf. And Charlie Walks Far was all right, too. Not as bright as Tom, but a hard worker and no trouble to anybody. It just didn't make sense that those two, of all the people in the county, red or white, would have swiped Bandelier's damned cigar company Indian. Not even as a prank, they were too sober-sided for that sort of foolishness.

It was a dozen miles out to the reservation, along a road that had been built for wagons, not Model T Fords. The motorcar was contrary at the best of times; on such a road as this it kept bucking and lurching, as if it didn't like my company or my hands on its steering wheel. By the time I drove onto reservation land, my backside was sorer than if I'd been sitting a saddle twenty-four hours straight.

The reservation was poor land, rocky and hilly, with almost no decent bottomland. No wonder Tom Black Wolf wanted to be an agronomist; you'd have to have special training, and maybe divine help, to grow worthwhile crops in soil like this. That was the federal government for you: force the Indians onto such land and then expect them to lick your boots in gratitude just because the land was free. It was a hell of a thing to be born with a skin color different than the men who run the country, particularly when the country had been yours in the first place.

Close to five hundred Indians lived here—Flatheads, mostly, with a few Piegans and Bloods. Their homes were slab-built shacks put up by the government back in the 'Seventies, most of them scattered around a small, shallow lake. There were some ramshackle barns and livestock pens—the Indians ran sheep, goats, and a few head of cattle—and an agency store and an infirmary where the poorly trained reservation doctor treated ills and disease with such medicines as the Bureau of Indian Affairs doled out. Tweaked my conscience every time I came out here, even though I'd had nothing to do with building the place or running it. It was squalor, plain and simple, two generations' worth, and no man worth his salt faces squalor with a clear conscience.

A dirt road rimmed the lake, and the flivver made so much noise rattling along it that kids and dogs ran and hid. When I came up to Chief Victor's house—bigger than most, as befitted his station—Tom Black Wolf appeared in the doorway. He watched me shut the motor down and climb out and walk on over to him. Usually he had a smile for me, but today he was all Indian; there wasn't any more expression on his lean face or in his eyes than there was in Henry Bandelier's wooden Indian.

I didn't smile, either. I said: " 'Morning, Tom. Taste of snow in the air, wouldn't you say?"

"Yes. Have you come to see me, Sheriff Monk?"

"Some questions I'd like to ask you. I don't want to disturb your grandfather, though. We can talk out here."

"Chief Victor has been moved to the infirmary. The doctor requested it two days ago."

"He's bad off, then?"

"Yes. It is almost his time."

"I'm sorry, Tom."

"You shouldn't be," he said. "It is only a passage. Chief Victor has led a long and honorable life, and he will find his reward." I nodded, and Tom said then, formal: "Please come inside where it's warm."

We went in. Tom kept the place clean, and mostly neat except for books. He was a reader, Tom was—read anything and everything, on just about any subject you could name. Hungry for knowledge, that was Tom Black Wolf. There were books on the wood block tables and chairs and scattered in piles over the painted board floor. Some were his, that he'd bought through mail order; others belonged to the new Elk Basin Lending Library. Miss Mary Ellen Belknap, the librarian and town historian, let him check out as many as he wanted, despite the few good citizens who frowned on such generosity.

I went over and stood by the stove to thaw myself out. Tom let me warm some before he said: "You have questions, you said?"

"It's a law matter. Seems that wooden Indian sets out in front of Henry Bandelier's store was stolen last night. He thinks you and Charlie Walks Far did the deed."

Tom didn't say anything.

"Did you, son? You and Charlie?"

He just looked at me with his face set and his lips pressed tightly together. That gave me another twinge, for it told me he was guilty, all right, and that he wasn't going to own up to it. An Indian who respects you—and I knew Tom respected me—won't lie to your face, the way a white man will. Instead, he keeps his mouth shut and lets you think whatever you like.

"Tom," I said, "stealing's a serious crime, you know that. Even if it is of a public eyesore. If you've got that wooden Indian around here somewhere, I'll find it. Go easier on you and Charlie if you tell me where it is and your reason for making off with it."

"You're welcome to search, Sheriff Lucas."

"Is that all you got to say?"

He nodded. Once.

"All right, then," I said. "I'll just go ahead and see what's what around here."

Which I did, and, of course, I didn't find any sign of that eight-foot chunk of wood. Finding it wasn't going to be *that* easy. When I was done, I walked with him to the flivver, and then stopped and turned and said: "You been doing some saw work this morning, Tom?"

It didn't faze him. Takes a better white man than me to surprise an Indian, I guess. He said, bland as you please: "Saw work?"

"Got sawdust all over your shoes." He did, too. I'd noticed it while I was warming up at the stove. "Don't look like cottonwood or jack pine or any other wood grows around here. Matter of fact, it looks like that tobacco-spit brown wood Henry Bandelier's statue is carved out of."

Tom didn't say anything.

"Cut it up for firewood, did you?"

Silence.

"Or maybe it offended you boys somehow. That it?"

Silence.

I sighed, though not so's he could hear me do it, and said—"Reckon I'll be back, Tom."—and got into the flivver.

I found Charlie Walks Far tending sheep on the hardscrabble land north of the lake. I had to leave the Ford on the road; if I'd tried to drive up to where Charlie was, I'd have busted an axle or bruised my liver or both. But I was just wasting my time. Charlie was as close-mouthed as Tom. No lies, no admissions, just civility and nothing more.

So then I went to see Abe Fetters, the Indian agent who also ran the reservation store. He didn't know anything about the wooden Indian—not that I expected him to—and said he just couldn't believe Tom Black Wolf and Charlie Walks Far would resort to common thievery. "Particularly not now," Abe went on, "with Chief Victor so sick. Why, it'd be an act of disrespect, and you know how Tom idolizes his grandfather."

"Maybe they had a good reason for it," I said.

"They may have thought so. But what?"

"Well, I don't know. Some ceremonial reason, maybe?"

Abe laughed without much humor. "Take my word for it," he said, "there's no Flathead ceremony involving a wooden Indian."

I asked him to help me comb the village and see what we could find. He said he would. And we did. And that was another big waste of time. Whatever Tom and Charlie had done with the statue, it was well hidden—or its remains were. We didn't find even a speck of sawdust to match the kind on Tom's shoes.

We stopped finally at the infirmary, for I thought it proper to pay my respects—likely my last respects—to Chief Victor. But the old man was asleep, and the half-breed doctor, Joshua Teel, wouldn't let me in to see him. Chief Victor likely wouldn't recognize me, anyway, Teel said. The old warrior was mostly delirious now and had been for a couple of days.

So it was a morning of frustrations all around.

Wasn't anything for me to do but drive on back to Elk Basin. It was well past noon by that time, and I was almost as hungry as I was puzzled. None of it made a lick of sense. Hell, if anything the theft made less sense now than it had before I'd visited the reservation. Why would two basically honest young Indians steal a worthless wooden Indian? And why in tarnation would they take a saw to it once they had?

Back in town I put the Model T away in the City Hall barn and then went and hunted up Lloyd Cooper and had a little talk with him. After which I took my sore bones to the Elite Café for a late lunch. But before I could eat it, Henry Bandelier came prancing in; he'd seen me drive through earlier, and he'd also seen that I was alone—no Tom Black Wolf, no Charlie Walks Far, and no wooden Indian.

"Well?" he demanded, after he'd sat down uninvited at my table. "Why didn't you arrest those two bucks?"

"I didn't arrest 'em," I said, "on account of I got no evidence they're the guilty parties."

"No evidence? Hogwash! I told you Lloyd Cooper saw them stealing my Indian in the middle of the night."

"That's not exactly what Lloyd saw. I just talked to him

myself a few minutes ago. He saw Tom and Charlie, all right, on board a wagon with something in the bed under a piece of canvas, but he didn't see what that something was. Not so much as a glimpse of it."

"It was my Indian. You know it was!"

"I don't know no such thing," I said. "I didn't find that statue of yours out at the reservation, nor anybody who knew anything about it."

Bandelier shaped his lips like a man about to spit. "Just how carefully did you search, Sheriff?"

"Carefully enough." I fixed him with a hard eye. "And I don't like your tone, Mister Bandelier. You implying that I haven't done my duty?"

"If the shoe fits," he said, prissy.

"Well, it don't fit," I said. "Now suppose you take yourself back behind your store counter and let me eat my lunch in peace and quiet."

"I'm warning you, Sheriff Monk. . . ."

"You're doing what?"

He didn't like what he saw in my face. He scraped back his chair, not meeting my eyes now, and said to my left shoulder: "If you don't do anything about those two thieving Flatheads, then I will."

"Such as?"

"That's my business."

"Not if it involves breaking the law. You do anything illegal, like going out to the reservation yourself with mischief in mind, and I'll cloud up and rain all over you. And you can damned well count on that."

I spoke loud, so that the five other citizens in the Elite could also hear my words plain. Bandelier's face got even redder than it already was. But he didn't sling any more words of his own; he put his back to me and walked out all still and righteous, like a sinner leaving a tent meeting.

Well, hell, I thought. Now I'd lost my appetite.

Henry Bandelier was born without the sense God gave a picket-pin gopher. He tried to stir up trouble in spite of my warning. He talked long and fast to anybody who'd listen about the "red heathens out on the reservation," and what low-down thieves they were, and, even though it had been years since we'd had any problems to speak of with the Indians, there were some hotheads who believed him. There'd have been an incident come out of it, too, with white men and red both getting hurt, if I hadn't got wind of a midnight meeting in the back of Bandelier's store. Half a dozen men were there, armed with axe handles and fortified with free liquor, and they were getting ready to ride on out to the reservation to "teach those Indians a lesson," as Bandelier was saying, when I busted in.

I chased the others home and threw Bandelier in jail on a charge of inciting to riot. He squawked long and loud, which was fine with me. So I added "threatening a peace officer with bodily harm" to the charges against him.

In the morning Bandelier demanded his lawyer. When Jack Dunlap showed up, I talked to him first, after which he consulted with Bandelier in private for the better part of an hour. What he said must have put the fear of God into the storekeeper; Bandelier was some subdued when we all went trooping over to see Judge Cooney. The judge let Bandelier out on bail, and I promised to reduce the charges against him on the proviso that he quit trying to provoke conflict with the Indians and leave the matter of the missing statue in the hands of the law.

That put an end to the trouble. Bandelier had too much self-esteem to suffer a public disgrace lightly; he retreated into his store and his humiliation, and from then on kept his big mouth shut.

I continued to investigate the theft, off and on, for two days, but there just wasn't anything to find out. I was considering another drive out to the reservation when Abe Fetters showed up in town with the news that Chief Victor had died.

I talked to Abe over at the train dépôt, where he was picking up a consignment of supplies from the government. He said the old man had passed on two nights ago, in his sleep. Yesterday there'd been the usual tribal ceremony presided over by the medicine man. Today, though, there'd been something that *wasn't* usual.

"What's that, Abe?" I asked.

"Well, the burial," he said. "They took his remains out to the burial ground before dawn without telling the medicine man. Or me, for that matter. I didn't find out until after it was already done."

"Who did?"

"Tom Black Wolf and members of his family. Funny breach of custom. First time anything like it has happened."

"Tom give you an explanation?"

"No," Abe said. "I asked him and so did the medicine man, but he wouldn't say. He must have had a good reason, though. Indians don't do anything without a good reason."

"You got any idea what it might be?"

"Not a one."

Neither did I, right then. But I sure did that evening.

The official part of my day ends at six o'clock, when my night deputy, Gus Beemis, comes on. Since I lost my wife Tess two years ago, my evenings tend to be pretty quiet and of a sameness. Usually I have supper at the Elite Café, go on home, do such chores as need doing, turn in, and read myself to sleep. Gets lonely sometimes, especially around the holidays, but a man learns to live with that, same as he learns to live with all the other things, good and bad, that make up his life.

Some evenings after supper I stop by the library before I head home, to pick up and return books. In my early days I wasn't much of a reader, but after Tess passed on, I took it up on a regular basis, just as Tom Black Wolf had, and found that I'd been short-changing myself most of my life. Books are more than just tools of knowledge; good books are friends. Better friends, some of them, than the human variety.

This was one of my nights to stop by the library. And I chanced to walk in while Mary Ellen Belknap was having a conversation with Lydia Cranston, Doc Cranston's wife. Indians was what they were talking about—Chief Victor's passing, at first. The library is small, so I couldn't have helped overhearing them if I'd wanted to. And I didn't want to when their talk shifted to Tom Black Wolf.

"I swan," Mary Ellen said, "I'll never understand Indians."

"Why do you say that?" Lydia asked.

"Well, you take Tom Black Wolf. He's always been such a good boy. Smart, well-mannered, and respectful of property. That's why I've let him check out books since he was in high school. He never abused the privilege. But now . . . well, I hope he isn't going to start running wild."

"Why would you think he'd start running wild, for heaven's sake?"

"It's the little things, isn't it?" Mary Ellen said. "That's how it always starts. And now that Chief Victor is gone, the authority figure in Tom's life. . . ."

"*What* little things?"

"The last batch of books he checked out were overdue for almost two weeks. He's never had overdue books before."

"Well, my land, with his grandfather so sick. . . ."

"That's not all," Mary Ellen said. "He also mutilated a book."

"He did what?"

"Mutilated a book. Don't look at me that way, Lydia, it's true. He tore a photograph out of an expensive history book. Oh, he pasted it back in, but you can see plainly where it was ripped out. . . ."

I was over at the desk by then. I said: "Mary Ellen, when did you find out about this torn photograph?"

She blinked at me. She's six feet tall and horse-faced, and, when she blinks, she looks like a startled mare. "Why . . . just this afternoon, Sheriff. Tom brought in the books that were overdue. One was the history text. . . ."

"You have that book handy?"

"Yes, it's on my desk."

"Mind letting me see it?"

"Of course not, but what . . . ?"

"Just let me see the book, Mary Ellen."

She got it for me. The title and subtitle were stamped in gilt on the front cover: SONS AND DAUGHTERS OF THE NILE: A HISTORY OF EGYPT FROM ANCIENT TO MODERN TIMES. I opened it up and found the photograph that had been torn out and pasted back in, and took a good long look at it, and that was when I got my notion. The damnedest notion I'd ever had, but there it was.

I said to Mary Ellen: "I'd like to borrow this book until tomorrow."

"Check it out, you mean? But it needs to be properly repaired. . . ."

"Just until tomorrow, Mary Ellen."

Before she could say anything else, I tucked the book under my arm and went on out. I could feel the two women's eyes on my back, and I could hear them start to whisper even before I shut the door.

When I got home, I sat in my Morris chair and did some studying on the history book. Then I did some studying without the book, working that notion of mine from different angles. And, by golly, all the pieces fit together as pretty as you please.

The missing wooden Indian . . . the sawdust on Tom's shoes the morning after the theft . . . Chief Victor's illness and delirium . . . Tom and his family not letting either the tribal medicine man or Abe Fetters come along to the burial grounds . . . and the torn-out photograph in the Egyptian history book—the photograph of a sarcophagus, one of those stone coffins made in the likeness of kings and queens and other royalty that were buried inside them.

Suppose Tom and Charlie Walks Far hadn't cut that wooden Indian into pieces; suppose they'd sawed it clean in half, lengthwise, and then hollowed out both halves with hammers and wood chisels. And suppose they'd put Chief Victor's remains inside and buried Indian and wooden Indian both.

Chief Victor himself would have had to ask for it. And he might have, even if it went smack against tribal custom, if he'd been addled enough in his sickness. Could be he'd got hold of the Egyptian history book—Tom always had books lying around their shack—and could be he'd seen that photograph of the sarcophagus, and torn it out because it fascinated him, and in his delirium determined that he was royalty, too, descended from the Great Chief Victor, so why shouldn't he have a coffin like the Egyptian royalty did? Tom wouldn't have refused anything his grandfather asked, no matter how daft or heretical; he'd likely have tried to argue against it, but in the end he wouldn't have refused. And since there was no time to build a sarcophagus in the old warrior's true likeness, with Chief Victor already knocking at death's door, Tom and Charlie Walks Far had had to make do with what came easy to hand.

But, hell, it was a crazy notion. Pure foolishness, even if all the pieces did fit. Must be some other explanation that made better and saner sense.

And yet. . . .

Well, I *could* tell Abe Fetters about it, and we *could* go out to the reservation burial ground and find out for certain. But that struck me as downright sacrilegious. Those poor Indians had enough trials and tribulations without a bunch of white men digging up their sacred burial ground. Besides which, if it did turn out to be true, then the citizens of Elk Basin would have a field day at the Indians' expense, and the whole thing would get written up in newspapers around the state and maybe around the country, too. And as if that wasn't bad enough, I'd have to arrest Tom and Charlie, and Henry Bandelier would sure as hell press charges against them. There'd be no justice in that. Tom couldn't go to the university and become an agronomist and help his people if he was serving a stretch in the state penitentiary.

No, I decided, the best thing for me to do was to keep that crazy notion of mine to myself. Better yet, dismiss it as a pipe dream and forget all about it.

That's just what I did. And to this day nobody in Elk Basin has ever found out what really happened to Henry Bandelier's wooden Indian. Including me. Some things, I reckon, folks are just better off not knowing.

Decision

The day was coming on dusk, the sky flame-streaked and the desert heat easing some, when I found the small hardscrabble ranch. It lay nestled within a broad ring of bluffs and cactus-strewn hillocks. Crouched beside a draw leading between two of the bluffs was a pole-and-'dobe cabin and two weathered outbuildings. Even from where I sat my steel dust high above, I could see that whoever lived there was not having an easy time of it. Heat had parched and withered the corn and other vegetables in the cultivated patch along one side, and the spare buildings looked to be crumbling, like the powdering bones of animals long dead.

There were no bones or other livestock in the open corral near the cabin, no sign of life anywhere. Except for the wisps of chimney smoke, rising pale and steady, the place had the look of abandonment. It was the smoke that had drawn me off El Camino Real del Diablo some minutes earlier, that and the fact that both my water bags were near empty.

Most days there seemed to be a fair amount of traffic on the Devil's Highway—the only good road between Tucson and Yuma, part of the Gila Trail that connected California with points east to Texas. Over the past week I'd come on pioneers, freighters, drifters, a Butterfield stagecoach, a company of soldiers on its way to Fort Yuma, groups of men looking for work on the rail line the Southern Pacific had begun building eastward from the Colorado River the previous year, 1878. But today, when I needed water and would have paid dear for it, the road had been deserted.

156

It was my own fault that I was low on water. I could have filled the bags when I passed through the town of Maricopa Wells last night, but I'd decided to keep on without stopping; it had been late enough so that even the saloons were closed, and I saw no need to go knocking on someone's door at that hour. It was my intention to buy water at the next way station for the Butterfield line, but when I got there, close to noon, the stationmaster had refused me. His main spring had gone bad, he said, and they had precious little for their own needs. He'd let me stay there for most of the afternoon, waiting in the shade by the corral. Not a soul had passed by the time I rode on again at five o'clock. And I had seen no one, either.

I hoped the people who lived down below had enough water to spare. If they didn't, I would have to go back to the Devil's Highway and do some more waiting; neither the steel dust nor I was fit enough for moving on without water. I could see the ranch's well set under a plank lean-to in the dusty yard, and I licked at my parched lips. Well, I had nothing to lose by riding down and asking.

I heeled the horse forward, sitting slack in the saddle. Even traveling mostly by night, and even though it was not yet the middle of May, a man dries out in the desert, wearies bone-deep. But the desert also had a way of dulling the mind, which was the reason I had decided to ride alone instead of traveling by coach through these Arizona badlands. I didn't want company or conversation because they would only lead to questions and then sharpened memories I did not care to dwell on. Memories that needed to be buried, the way I had buried Emma four months and six days ago in the sun-webbed ground outside Lordsburg.

People I knew there, friends, said the pain would go away after a while. All you had to do was to keep on living the best you could, and time would help you forget—forget how she'd collapsed one evening after a dozen hours' hard toil on our own hardscrabble land, and how I'd thought it was just the ague because she'd been complaining of chest pains, and that terrible time when I came back from town with the doctor and found her lying in our bed so still and small, not breathing, gone. Heart failure, the doctor said. Twenty-eight years old, prime of life, and her good heart had betrayed her.

Maybe they were right, the friends who'd given their advice. But four months and six days of living the best I could hadn't eased the grief inside me, not with everything and everyone in Lordsburg reminding me of Emma. So a week ago I had sold the farm, packed a few changes of clothing and some personal belongings and a spare pistol into my saddlebags, and set out west into Arizona Territory. I had no idea where I was going or what I would do when the hundred and eighty dollars I carried in my boot dwindled away. I had nothing, and I wanted nothing except to drift through the long days and longer nights until life took on some meaning again, if it ever would.

The trail leading down to the ranch was steep and switchbacked in places, and it took me the better part of twenty minutes to get to where the buildings were. The harsh daylight had softened by then, and the tops of the bluffs seemed to have turned a reddish-purple color; the sky looked flushed now, instead of brassy the way it did at midday.

I rode slowly toward the cabin, keeping my hands up and in plain sight. Desert settlers, being as isolated as they were, would likely be mistrustful of leaned-down, dust-caked strangers. When I reached the front yard, I drew rein. It was quiet there, and I still wasn't able to make out sound or movement at any of the buildings. Beyond the vegetable patch, a sagging utility shed stood with a padlock on its door; the only other structure was a long pole-sided shelter at the rear of the empty corral. In back of the shed, rows of pulque cactus stood like sentinels in the hot, dry earth.

I looked at the well, running my tongue through the dryness inside my mouth. Then I eased the steel dust half a rod closer to the cabin and called out: "Hello, the house!"

Silence.

"Hello! Anybody home?"

There was more silence for a couple of seconds, and I was thinking of stepping down. But then a woman's voice said from inside: "What do you want here?" It was a young voice, husky, but dulled by something I couldn't identify. The door was closed and the front window was curtained in monk's cloth, but I sensed that the woman was standing by the window, watching me through the curtain fabric.

"Don't be alarmed, ma'am," I said. "I was wondering if you could spare a little water. I'm near out."

She didn't answer. Silence settled again, and I began to get a vague feeling of something being wrong. It made me shift uncomfortably in the saddle.

"Ma'am?"

"I can't let you have much," she said finally.

"I'll pay for whatever you can spare."

"You won't need to pay."

"That's kind of you."

"You can step down if you like."

I put on a smile and swung off and slapped some of the fine powdery dust off my shirt and Levi's. The door opened a crack, but she didn't come out.

"My name is Jennifer Todd," she said from inside. "My husband and I own this ranch." She spoke the word "husband" as if it were a blasphemy.

"I'm Roy Boone," I said.

"Mister Boone." And she opened the door and moved out

into the fading light.

My smile vanished; I stared at her with my mouth coming open. She was no more than twenty, hair the color of near-ripe corn and piled in loose braids on top of her head, eyes brown and soft and wide—pretty eyes. But it wasn't any of this that caused me to stare as I did. It was the blue-black bruises on both sides of her face, the deep cut above her right brow, the swollen, mottled surface of her upper lip and her right temple.

"Jesus God!" I said. "Who did that to you, Missus Todd?"

"My husband. This morning, just before he left for Maricopa Wells."

"But *why?*"

"He was hung-over," she said. "Pulque hung over. Mase is mean when he's sober and meaner when he's drunk, but when he's bad hung over, he's the devil's own child."

"He's done this to you before?"

"More times than I can count."

"Maybe I've no right to say this, but why don't you leave him? Missus Todd, a man who'd do a thing like this to a woman wouldn't hesitate to kill her if he was riled enough."

"I tried to leave him," she said. "I tried it three times. He came after me each time and brought me back here and beat me half crazy. A work animal's got sense enough to obey if it's whipped enough times."

I could feel the anger inside me. I was thinking of Emma again, the love we'd had, the tenderness. Some men never knew or understood feelings like that; some men gave only one kind of pain, never felt the other kind, deep inside them. They never realized what they had with a good woman. Or cared. Men like that. . . .

Impulsively I put the rest of the thought into words. "A

man like that ought to be shot dead for what he's done to you."

Something flickered in her eyes, and she said: "If I had a gun, Mister Boone, I expect I'd do just that thing . . . I'd shoot him, with no regrets. But there's only one rifle and one pistol, and Mase carries them with him during the day. At night he locks them up in the shed yonder."

It made me feel uneasy to hear a woman talking so casually about killing. I looked away from her, wondering if it was love or some other reason that had made her marry this Mase Todd, somebody who kept her like a prisoner in a badlands valley, who beat her and tried to break her.

When I looked back at Mrs. Todd, she smiled in a fleeting, humorless way. "I don't know what's the matter with me, telling you all my troubles. You've problems of your own, riding alone across the desert. Come inside. I've some stew on the fire, and you can take an early supper with me if you like."

"Ma'am, I. . . ."

"Mase won't be home until late tonight or tomorrow morning, if you're thinking of him."

"I wasn't, no. He doesn't worry me."

"You look tired and hungry," she said, "and we don't get many visitors out here. I've no one to talk to most days. I'd take it as a kindness if you'd accept."

I couldn't find a way to refuse her. I just nodded and let her show me inside the cabin.

It was filled with shadows and smelled of spiced jackrabbit stew and boiling coffee. The few pieces of furniture were hand-hewn, but whoever had made them—likely her husband—had done a poor, thoughtless job; none of the pieces looked as though it would last much longer. But the two rooms I saw were clean and straightened, and you could see that she'd done the best she could with what she had, that she'd tried to make a home out of it.

She lighted a mill lantern on the table to chase away some of the shadows. Then she said: "There's water in that basin by the hearth, if you want to wash up. I'll fetch some drinking water from the well, and I'll see to your horse."

"You needn't bother yourself. . . ."

"It's no bother."

She turned and went to the door, walking in a stiff, slow way but holding herself erect; her spirit wasn't broken yet. I watched her go out and shut the door behind her, and I thought: *She's some woman. Most would be half-dead shells by now if they'd gone through what she has.*

I crossed to the basin, washed with a cake of strong yellow soap. Mrs. Todd came back as I was drying off. She handed me a gourd of water, and, while I drank from it, she unhooked a heavy iron kettle from a spit rod suspended above a banked fire. She spooned stew onto tin plates, poured coffee, set out a pan of fresh corn bread.

We ate mostly in silence. Despite what she'd said about not having anyone to talk to, she seemed not to want conversation. But there was something I needed to say, and, when I was done eating, I got it said.

"Missus Todd, you've been more than generous to share your food and water with me. I can't help feeling there must be something I can do for you."

"No, Mister Boone. There's nothing you can do."

"Well, suppose I just stayed until your husband gets home, had a little talk with him . . . ?"

"That wouldn't be wise," she said. "If Mase comes home and finds a strange man, he wouldn't wait to ask who you are or why you're here. He'd make trouble for you, and afterward he'd make more trouble for me."

What could I do? It was her property, her life, this was

business between her and her husband. If she'd asked for help, that would have been another matter. But she'd made her position clear. I had no right to force myself on her.

Outside, in the moon-washed purple of early evening, I thanked her again and tried to offer her money for the food and water. But she wouldn't have any of it. She was too proud to take payment for hospitality. She insisted that I fill my water bags from the well before riding out, so I lowered the wooden bucket on the windlass and did that.

As I rode slowly out of the yard, I turned in the saddle to look back. She was still standing there by the well, looking after me, her hands down at her sides. In the silvery moonlight, she had a forlorn, fixed appearance—as if she had somehow taken root in the desert soil.

An hour later I was once again on the Devil's Highway, headed west. And a mounting sense of uneasiness had come to ride with me. For the first time in four months and six days, someone other than Emma was disturbing my thoughts. Jennifer Todd.

Like an echo in my mind, I heard some of the words she had spoken to me: *If I had a gun, Mister Boone, I expect I'd do just that thing . . . I'd shoot him, with no regrets. But there's only one rifle and one pistol, and Mase carries them with him during the day.*

I listened to the echo of those words, and I thought about the way she'd been watching me inside the cabin when I first rode in, the way she'd suddenly opened the door and come outside. Why had she come out at all? Beaten the way she was, most women would have stayed in the privacy of the cabin rather than allow a stranger to see them that way. And why had she talked so freely about her husband, about the kind of man he was?

163

Then I heard other words she'd spoken—*I'll fetch some drinking water from the well, and I'll see to your horse.*—and I drew sharp rein, swung quickly out of the saddle. I fumbled at the straps on the saddlebags, pulled them open, groped inside.

My spare six-gun was missing.

And along with it, three or four cartridges.

I stood there in the moonlight, leaning against the steel dust's flank, and I knew exactly what she had begun planning when she saw me ride in, and what she was planning when her husband came home from Maricopa Wells and tried to lay hand on her again. And yet, I couldn't raise anger for what she'd done. She had been driven to it. She had every right to protect herself.

But was it really self-defense? Or was it cold-blooded murder?

In the saddle again, I thought: *I've got to stop her.* Only then Emma came crowding into my thoughts again. Gone now—gone too young. So many years never to be lived, so many things never to be done; the child we had tried so hard to have never to be born. There had been nothing I could do to save her. But there was something I could do for another suffering young woman on another hardscrabble ranch.

I made my decision.

I kept on riding west.

Fear

He sat with his back to the wall, waiting.

Shadows shrouded the big room, thinned by early daylight filtering in through the plate-glass front window. Beyond the glass he could see Boxelder's empty main street, rain spattering the puddled mud that wagon wheels and horses' hoofs had churned into a quagmire. Wind rattled the chain-hung sign on the outer wall: **R. J. Cable, Saddle Maker**.

Familiar shapes surrounded him in the gloom. Workbenches littered with scraps of leather, mallets, cutters, stamping tools. A few saddles, finished and unfinished—not half as many as there used to be. Wall racks hung with bridles and hackamores, saddlebags and other accessories. Once the tools and accomplishments of his trade had given him pleasure, comfort, a measure of peace. Not any more. Even the good odors of new leather and beeswax and harness oil had soured in his nostrils.

It was cold in the shop; he hadn't bothered to lay a fire when he had come in at dawn, after another sleepless night. But he took little notice of the chill. He had been cold for a long while now, the kind of gut cold that no fire can ever thaw.

His hands, twisted together in his lap, were sweating.

He glanced over at the closed door to the storeroom. A seed company calendar was tacked to it—not that he needed a calendar to tell him what day this was. October 26, 1892. The day after Lee Tarbeaux was scheduled to be released from Deer Lodge Prison. The day Tarbeaux would return to

165

Boxelder after eight long years. The day Tarbeaux had vowed to end Reed Cable's life.

His gaze lingered on the storeroom door a few seconds longer. The shotgun was back there—his father's old double-barreled Remington that he'd brought from home yesterday—propped in a corner, waiting as he was. He thought about fetching it, setting it next to his stool. But there was no need yet. It was still early.

He scrubbed his damp palms on his Levi's, then fumbled in a vest pocket for his turnip watch. He flipped the dust-cover, held the dial up close to his eyes. Ten after seven. How long before Tarbeaux came? Noon at the earliest. There were a lot of miles between here and Deer Lodge. If he could work, it would make the time go by more quickly . . . but he couldn't. His hands were too unsteady for leather craft. It would be an effort to keep them steady enough to hold the shotgun when the time came.

A few more hours, he told himself. *Just a few more hours. Then it'll finally be over.* He sat watching the rain-swept street. Waiting.

It was a quarter past twelve when Lee Tarbeaux reached the outskirts of Boxelder. The town had grown substantially since he'd been away—even more than he'd expected. There were more farms and small ranches in the area, too—parcels deeded off to homesteaders where once there had been nothing but rolling Montana grassland. *Everything changes, sooner or later,* he thought as he rode. *Land, towns, and men, too. Some men.*

He passed the cattle pens near the railroad dépôt, deserted now in the misty rain. He'd spent many a day there when he had worked for Old Man Kendall—and one day in particular that he'd never forget, because it had been the beginning of the end of his freedom for eight long years. Kendall was dead now, died in his sleep in 'Eighty-Nine. Tarbeaux had been sorry to hear it, weeks after it had happened, on the prison grapevine. He'd held no hard feelings toward the old cowman or his son Bob. The Kendalls were no different from the rest of the people here; they'd believed Cable's lies and that there was a streak of larceny in Tarbeaux's kid-wildness. You couldn't blame them for feeling betrayed. Only one man to blame and that was Reed Cable.

Tarbeaux rode slowly, savoring the chill October air with its foretaste of winter snow. The weather didn't bother him, and it didn't seem to bother the spavined blue roan he'd bought cheap from a hostler in the town of Deer Lodge—something of a surprise, given the animal's age and condition. Just went to show that you couldn't always be sure about anybody or anything, good or bad. Except Reed Cable. Tarbeaux was sure Cable was the same man he'd been eight years ago. Bits and pieces of information that had filtered through the prison walls added weight to his certainty.

Some of the buildings flanking Montana Street were familiar: the Boxelder Hotel, the sprawling bulk of Steinmetz Brewery. Many others were not. It gave him an odd, uncomfortable feeling to know this town and yet not know it—to be home and yet to understand that it could never be home again. He wouldn't stay long. Not even the night. And once he left, he'd never come back. Boxelder, like Deer Lodge, like all his foolish kid plans, were part of a past he had to bury completely if he was to have any kind of future.

A chain-hung shingle, dancing in the wind, appeared in the gray mist ahead: **R. J. Cable, Saddle Maker**. The plate-glass window below the sign showed a rectangle of lamplight, even though there was a **Closed** sign in one corner. Tarbeaux barely glanced at the window as he passed, with no effort to see through the water-pocked glass. There was plenty of time. Patience was just one of the things his stay in the penitentiary had taught him. Besides, he was hungry. It had been hours since his meager trailside breakfast.

He tied the roan to a hitch rail in front of an eatery called the Elite Café. It was one of the new places; no one there knew or recognized him. He ordered hot coffee and a bowl of chili. And, as he ate, he thought about the things that drive a man, that shape and change him for better or worse. Greed was one. Hate was another. He knew all about hate; he'd lived with it a long time. But it wasn't the worst of the ones that ate the guts right out of a man. The worst was fear.

When Cable saw the lone, slicker-clad figure ride by outside, he knew it was Lee Tarbeaux. Even without a clear look at the man's face, shielded by the tilt of a rain hat, he knew. He felt a taut relief. It wouldn't be much longer now.

He extended a hand to the shotgun propped beside his stool. He'd brought it out of the storeroom two hours ago, placed it within easy reach. The sick feeling inside him grew and spread as he rested the weapon across his knees. His damp palms made the metal surfaces feel greasy. He kept his hands on it just the same.

His thoughts drifted as he sat there, went back again, as they so often did these days, to the spring of 'Eighty-Four. Twenty years old that spring, him and Lee Tarbeaux both. Friendly enough because they'd grown up together, both of them town kids, but not close friends. Too little in common. Too much spirit in Tarbeaux and not enough spirit in him. Lee went places and did things he was too timid to join in on.

When Tarbeaux turned eighteen, he'd gone to work as a hand on Old Man Kendall's K-Bar Ranch. He'd always had a reckless streak, and it had widened out over the following two years, thanks to a similar streak in Old Man Kendall's son Bob. Drinking, whoring, a few saloon fights. No serious trouble to make the law aware of Lee Tarbeaux.

Not a whisper of wildness in Reed Cable, meanwhile. Quiet and steady—that was what everyone said about him. Quiet and steady and honest. He took a position as night clerk at the Boxelder Hotel. Not because he wanted the job, saddle making and leatherwork were what he craved to do with his life. But there were two saddle makers in town already, and neither was interested in hiring an apprentice. He'd have moved to another town except that his ma, who'd supported them since his father's death, had taken sick and was no longer able to work as a seamstress. All up to him, then. And the only decent job he could find was the night clerk's.

Ma'd died in March of that year. One month after Tarbeaux's aunt—the last of his relatives—passed away. And on a day in late April Bob Kendall and Lee Tarbeaux and the rest of the K-Bar crew drove their roundup beeves in to the railroad loading pens. Old Man Kendall wasn't with them; he'd been laid up with gout. Bob Kendall was in charge, but he was a hammerhead as well as half wild: liquor and women and stud poker were all he cared about. Tarbeaux was with him when the cattle buyer from Billings finished his tally and paid off in cash. Seventy-four hundred dollars, all in greenbacks.

It was after bank closing hours by the time the deal was done. Bob Kendall hadn't cared to go hunting banker Weems to take charge of the money. He wanted a running start on his night's fun, so he turned the chore over to Lee. Tarbeaux made a half-hearted attempt to find the banker, and then his own itch got the best of him. He went to the hotel, where his old friend Reed had just come on shift, where the lobby was otherwise deserted, and laid the saddlebags full of money on the counter.

"Reed," he said without explanation, "do me a favor and put these bags in the hotel safe for tonight. I or Bob Kendall'll be back to fetch 'em the first thing in the morning."

It was curiosity that made him open the bags after Tarbeaux left. The sight of all that cash weakened his knees, dried his mouth. He put the saddlebags away in the safe, but he couldn't stop thinking about the money. So many things he could do with it, so many ambitions he could make a reality. A boldness and a recklessness built in him for the first time. The money grew from a lure into a consuming obsession as the hours passed. He might've been able to overcome it if his mother had still been alive, but he was all alone—with no prospects for the future and no one to answer to but himself.

He took the saddlebags from the safe an hour past midnight. Took them out back of the hotel stables and hid them in a clump of buck brush. Afterward he barely remembered doing it, as if it had all happened in a dream.

Bob Kendall came in alone at eight in the morning, hung over and in mean spirits, just as the day clerk arrived to serve as a witness. There was a storm inside Reed Cable, but outwardly he was calm. Saddlebags? He didn't know anything about saddlebags full of money. Tarbeaux hadn't been in last evening, no matter what he claimed. He hadn't seen Lee in more than two weeks.

In a fury Bob Kendall ran straight to the sheriff, and the sheriff arrested Tarbeaux. The hardest part of the whole thing was facing Lee, repeating the lies, and watching the outraged disbelief in Tarbeaux's eyes turn to blind hate. But the money was all he let himself think about. The money, the money, the money. . . .

It was his word against Tarbeaux's, his reputation against

Tarbeaux's. The sheriff believed him, the Kendalls believed him, the townspeople believed him—and the judge and jury believed him. The verdict was guilty, the sentence a minimum of eight years at hard labor.

Tarbeaux had made his vow of vengeance as he was being led from the courtroom. "You won't get away with this, Reed!" he yelled. "You'll pay and pay dear. As soon as I get out, I'll come back and make sure you pay!"

The threat had shaken Cable at the time. But neither it nor his conscience had bothered him for long. Tarbeaux's release from Deer Lodge was in the far future; why worry about it? He had the money, he had his plans—and, when one of the town's two saddle makers died suddenly of a stroke, he soon realized the first of his ambitions. . . .

Cable shifted position on the hard stool. That was then and this was now, he thought bitterly. The far future had become the present. Pain moved through his belly and chest; a dry cough racked him. He sleeved sweat from his eyes, peered again through the front window. A few pedestrians hurried by on the wet sidewalk; none was Lee Tarbeaux.

"Come on," he said aloud. "Come on, damn you, and get it over with!"

Tarbeaux finished his meal, took out the makings, and rolled a smoke to savor the final cup of coffee. Food, coffee, tobacco—it all tasted good again, now that he was free. He'd rushed through the first twenty years of his life, taking everything for granted. And he'd struggled and pained his way through the last eight, taking nothing for granted. He'd promised himself that, when he got out, he'd make his remaining years pass as slowly as he could, that he'd take the time to look and feel and learn, and that he'd cherish every minute of every new day.

He paid his bill, crossed the street to Adams Mercantile—another new business run by a stranger—and replenished his supplies of food and tobacco. That left him with just three dollars of his prison savings. He'd have to settle some place soon, at least long enough to take a job and build himself a stake. After that . . . no hurry, wherever he went and whatever he did. No hurry at all.

First things first, though. The time had come to face Reed Cable.

He felt nothing as he walked upstreet to where the chain-hung sign rattled and danced. It had all been worked out in his mind long ago. All that was left was the settlement.

Lamplight still burned behind the saddlery's window. Without looking through the glass, without hesitation, Tarbeaux opened the door and went in under a tinkling bell.

Cable sat on a stool at the back wall, an old double-barreled shotgun across his knees. He didn't move as Tarbeaux shut the door behind him. In the pale lamp glow Cable seemed small and shrunken. His sweat-stained skin was sallow, pinched, and his hands trembled. He'd aged twenty years in the past eight—an old man before his thirtieth birthday.

The shotgun surprised Tarbeaux a little. He hadn't figured on a willingness in Cable to put up a fight. He said as he took off his rain hat: "Expecting me, I see."

"I knew you'd come. You haven't changed much, Lee."

"Sure I have. On the inside. Just the opposite with you."

"You think so?"

"I know so. You fixing to shoot me with the scatter-gun?"

"If you try anything, I will."

"I'm not armed."

"Expect me to believe that?"

Tarbeaux shrugged and glanced slowly around the shadowed room. "Pretty fair leatherwork," he said. "Seems you were cut out to be a saddle maker, like you always claimed."

"Man's got to do something."

"That's a fact. Only thing is, he ought to do it with honest money."

"All right," Cable said.

"You admitting you stole the K-Bar money, Reed? No more lies?"

"Not much point in lying to you."

"How about the sheriff and Bob Kendall? Ready to tell them the truth, too . . . get it all off your chest?"

Cable shook his head. "It's too late for that."

"Why?"

"I couldn't face prison, that's why. I couldn't stand it."

"I stood it for eight years," Tarbeaux said. "It's not so bad, once you get used to it."

"No. I couldn't, not even for a year."

"Man can be in prison even when there's no bars on his windows."

Cable made no reply.

"What I mean, it's been a hard eight years for you, too. Harder, I'll warrant, than the ones I lived through. Isn't that so?"

Still no reply.

"It's so," Tarbeaux said. "You got yourself this shop and you learned to be a saddle maker. But then it all slid downhill from there. Starting with Clara Weems. You always talked about marrying her someday, having three or four kids . . . your other big ambition. But she turned you down when you asked for her hand. Married that storekeeper in Billings, instead."

The words made Cable's hands twitch on the shotgun. "How'd you know that?"

"I know plenty about you, Reed. You proposed to two other women. They wouldn't have you, either. Then you lost four thousand dollars on bad mining stock. Then one of your horses kicked over a lantern and burned down your barn and half your house. Then you caught consumption and were laid up six months during the winter of 'Ninety-One. . . ."

"That's enough," Cable said, but there was no heat in his voice. Only a kind of desperate weariness.

"No, it's not. Your health's been poor ever since, worsening steadily, and there's nothing much the sawbones can do about it. How much more time do they give you . . . four years? Five?"

"Addled, whoever told you that. I'm healthy enough. I've got a long life ahead of me."

"Four years . . . five, at the most. *I'm* the one with the long life ahead. And I aim to make it a good life. You remember how I could barely read and write? Well, I learned in prison, and now I can do both better than most. I learned a trade, too. Blacksmithing. One of these days I'll have my own shop, same as you, with my name on a sign out front bigger than yours."

"But first you had to stop here and settle with me."

"That's right. First I have to settle with you."

"Kill me, like you swore in court you'd do. Shoot me dead."

"I never swore that."

"Same as."

"You think I still hate you that much?"

"Don't you?"

"No," Tarbeaux said. "Not any more."

"I don't believe that. You're lying."

"You're the liar, Reed, not me."

"You want me dead. Admit it . . . you want me dead."

"You'll be dead in four or five years."

"You can't stand to wait that long. You want me dead here and now."

"No. All I ever wanted was to make sure you paid for what you did to me. Well, you're paying and paying dear. I came here to tell you to your face that I know you are. That's the only reason I came, the only settlement I'm after."

"You bastard, don't fool with me. Draw your gun and get it over with."

"I told you, I'm not armed."

Cable jerked the scatter-gun off his knees, a gesture that was meant to be provoking. But the muzzle wobbled at a point halfway between them, held there. "Make your play!"

Tarbeaux understood, then. There was no fight in Cable; there never had been. There was only fear. He said: "You're trying to *make* me kill you. That's it, isn't it? You want me to put you out of your misery."

It was as if he'd slapped Cable across the face. Cable's head jerked; he lurched to his feet, swinging the Remington until its twin muzzles were like eyes centered on Tarbeaux's face.

Tarbeaux stood motionless. "You can't stand the thought of living another five sick, hurting years, but you don't have the guts to kill yourself. You figured you could goad me into doing it for you."

"No. Make your play or I'll blow your god-damn' head off!"

"Not with that scatter-gun. It's not loaded, Reed. We both know that now."

Cable tried to stare him down. The effort lasted no more than a few seconds; his gaze slid down to the useless shotgun. Then, as if the weight of the weapon was too much for his shaking hands, he let it fall to the floor, kicked it clattering under one of the workbenches.

175

"Why?" he said in a thin, hollow whisper. "Why couldn't you do what you vowed you'd do? Why couldn't you finish it?"

"It is finished," Tarbeaux said.

And it was, in every way. Now he really was free—of Cable and the last of his hate, of the past. Now he could start living again.

He turned and went out into the cold, sweet rain.

Cable slumped again onto his stool. Tarbeaux's last words seemed to hang like a frozen echo in the empty room.

It is finished.

For Tarbeaux, maybe it was. Not for Reed Cable. It wouldn't be finished for him for a long, long time.

"Damn you," he said, and then shouted the words. "Damn you!" But they weren't meant for Lee Tarbeaux this time. They were meant for himself.

He kept on sitting there with his back to the wall.

Waiting.

Not a Lick of Sense

We come down out of the high country some past sunup, Lige driving the wagon too dang' fast. Winter had played hob with the track, still had snow on it, deep in places. Every time a wheel jounced into a chuckhole or rut, the big old pine-board outhouse tied onto the bed swayed and creaked and groaned.

I kept hollering at him to slow down. Didn't do no good. When he latches onto some notion, he's like a mule with its teeth in a bale of hay. He don't have a lick of sense, Lige don't. I'm the Hovey born with all the sense; he's the one born with all the stubborn.

"Quit your bellerin'," he said once. "That outhouse ain't gonna bust loose and go flyin'. She's roped in tight."

"That ain't what's worryin' me."

"Won't shake apart, not as solid as we built her."

"Ain't that, neither, and you know it."

"All the more reason to get this here business over with quick. I still ain't sure we ought to be doin' it."

"After all the work we done? Lige, sometimes you're a pure fool."

"Wes," he said, "sometimes you're another."

I breathed some easier when we come to the junction with the county road. Off east was Antelope Valley and the Piegan Indian reservation. Little Creek was four miles to the west, and I had me a wish it was where we was headed right now. After four months up in the high country, we was near out of supplies. And I could scarce recall my last visit to Miss Sally's sporting house behind the Red Rock Saloon.

177

Lige turned us east. Wasn't near so cold down on the flats, though I could still see the frost of my breath and Lige's and our roan horse Jingalee's. No drifts of snow left on the ground, neither, like up to our place. You could smell things growing again, and about time, too. It'd sure been a long, hard winter.

County road wasn't near as bad off as the mountain track, and Lige commenced to push Jingalee even harder. I hollered at him, but he didn't pay me no mind. Not a lick of sense, by grab. That poor horse was showing lather already, and we still had us a distance left to travel. . . .

"Oh, Lordy Lord!" Lige said, sudden. "Wes, look yonder."

I looked. Man on horseback had just come trotting around a bend ahead. He was all bundled up in a sheepskin greatcoat and a neck muffler, his hat pulled down low, but I knowed him and that steel dust of his right off. So did Lige. Morgan Conagher, sheriff of Little Creek.

"What in tarnation's *he* doin' out here this early?" I said.

"Gonna ask us the same thing." Lige hauled back on the reins some and then give me one of his hot looks, all smoke and sparks. "You and your ideas," he said.

"Ain't nothing wrong with my ideas. You just let me do the talkin', hear?"

He muttered something and slowed us to a rocking stop as Conagher rode up alongside. He was a big 'un, Morgan was, and a holy terror with fists and six-gun, both. Smart, too, for a lawman. Unless a man was plain simple, he walked and talked soft when his path crossed Morgan Conagher's.

" 'Morning, boys," he said. "Cold as a gambler's eyeball, ain't it?"

"For a fact. Warmer than up to our place, though."

"Long time since I seen you two. Snowed in most of the winter?"

"Since the first week of December. How come you to be out riding this early, Mister Conagher?"

"Spent the night at Hank Staggs's place in the valley. Little trouble out there yesterday."

"Serious?"

"Not so's you'd notice. Hank figured he had a gripe against a couple of Piegan braves. Turned out to be the other way around." Conagher took his corncob pipe outen a coat pocket and commenced to chewing on the stem. Pipe bowl was black, but I'd never seen him smoke the thing. Gnawing the stem seemed to satisfy him the same as tobacco. "Now that's a curious sight," he said.

"What is?"

"Thing you got tied in your wagon there. Looks like an outhouse."

"Well, that's what she is, all right."

"Can't mistake that half-moon cut in the door."

"No, sir, sure can't."

"Takin' it out for an airing, are you?"

Lige, who don't have no more humor in him than he does sense, just set there. But I laughed before I said: "Be a couple of jugheads if that's what we was doing, wouldn't we, Sheriff? No, the fact is. . . ."

"Fact is," Lige said before I could get anything else out, "we're takin' her over to Charley Hammond's place."

"That so?" Conagher said. "What for?"

Damn Lige for a fool! I give him a sidewise glance and a sharp kick with the toe of my boot, both by way of telling him to put a hitch on his fat lip, but he went right on blabbering.

"She don't set the ground right," he said, "and she's got chinks and warped boards. Wind comes whistlin' through them chinks on a cold night, it like to freeze you where you sit."

"Uhn-huh."

"Well, Charley's the best carpenter in the county," Lige said. "So we figured to take her over and let him fix her up."

"Seems like a lot of work for you boys. Been easier to've had Charley bring his tools up to your ranch."

"Sure it would. But he's gettin' on in years, and we're askin' a favor, so we come to the notion of bringin' her down to the valley instead."

Conagher nodded and chewed his pipe stem, and I began to have the hope he'd ride on and leave us be. But then he said: "How come you closed off the bottom end?"

"Sheriff?"

"Bottom end there. Closed it off with canvas, didn't you? Canvas over boards, I'd say."

"Well, now," Lige said, and then he just set there, the big jughead, on account of he couldn't think of no good answer.

"Tell you how it looks to me," Conagher said. "Looks like you boys built yourself a big packing case out of your outhouse. Now why would you go and do a thing like that?"

"Sheriff," I said, "it ain't no use tryin' to fool you. Lige and me done closed off that bottom end, right enough, but it wasn't to make a packing case. No, sir. It was something else entire we made outen that outhouse."

"Such as?"

"A coffin. We built us a coffin."

"Coffin?" Conagher frowned and chewed his pipe stem, and then he said: "Who for?"

"Old Bryce. Our hired man."

"Mean to tell me you got *him* inside there?"

"His poor froze-stiff remains, yes, sir. He up and died two nights ago. Had him the ague and it turned into new-monia, and he up and died on us. Man weighed three hundred pounds, if he weighed an ounce . . . you know how big he was, Sheriff. So there we was with a three-hundred-pound, six-foot-and-three-inch-high corpse and no way to give him a proper Christian burial."

"How come no way? Ground still froze at your place?"

"Froze hard as stone," I said. "That's one reason we couldn't plant old Bryce. Other one is, we didn't have no wood left to build a coffin. No lumber a-tall. Winter was so long and cold, we run out of stove wood and had to burn up the last of our lumber to keep warm."

"I thought you boys always took pains to provision yourselves against long winters. Got a reputation for laying in plenty of food, plenty of wood."

"That's just what we do, usual, Mister Conagher. But this winter we got caught short. Had us a lean year, last, and the first blizzard took us unawares, and next thing we knowed, we was snowed in. Why, we was just about ready to chop up that there outhouse and burn *it*. Would have if the weather hadn't finally broke. And then old Bryce up and died on us."

"Uhn-huh."

"Big and tall as he was, why, he fits inside there just about snug. Couldn't have hammered up a better coffin from scratch. . . ."

"Where you fixing to bury him?"

"Sheriff?"

"Old Bryce in his outhouse coffin. Where you intend to put him down for his final resting place? Town cemetery's in the other direction."

"Yes, sir, that's right, so it is."

"Well?"

Lige had that hot look in his eyes again; he kicked me down low on the shin where Conagher couldn't see. But I wasn't about to just set there like him. I said: "Potter's fishing hole."

"Bury a dead man in a fishing hole?"

"No, sir, not in Potter's hole. Near it. That was old Bryce's favorite spot in all of Montana. He spent every free chance he had down at Potter's fishing hole, and that's a fact."

"Uhn-huh."

"Well, right before he croaked on us, he said as how he'd like to be buried down by Potter's fishing hole. Didn't he, Lige?"

Lige had enough sense to nod his head. Scowl on his ugly face said he was of a mind to gnaw my innards the way Conagher was gnawing his pipe stem.

"Can't deny a man his dying wish," I said. "So me and Lige, we pulled the outhouse down and put old Bryce into her and closed off her bottom and now we're headed down to Potter's to find a shady spot to plant 'em both."

"How you figure on doing the planting?"

"Sheriff?"

"I don't see any tools in that wagon bed."

"Tools?"

"No pick, no shovel. Not even a hoe. Was you boys thinking of digging old Bryce's grave with your bare hands?"

"Lordy Lord," Lige said, disgusted, and spat out onto the road. Done it too close to Jingalee; roan horse hopped forward a couple of steps before Lige hauled him down again. When that happened, the outhouse lurched and swayed some—same as my insides was doing right then.

"Well?"

"Well, now, Mister Conagher, sir. . . ."

"Time you untied those ropes," he said.

"Sheriff?"

"You and your brother. Untie those ropes and we'll have a squint inside that outhouse."

"Ain't nothing to see except old Bryce's froze-stiff corpse. . . ."

"Untie, boys. Now."

182

Wasn't nothing else we could do. Conagher was wearing his official holy terror look now, and his hand was setting on the butt of his Judge Colt. Lige kicked me again, twice, while we was taking off the ropes; I just let him do it.

"Open up that half-moon door, Wes."

I opened it, and Conagher poked around inside. A smile come to his mouth like a hungry wolf with supper waiting. "Well, well," he said. "Sure don't appear to be old Bryce's remains to me. What's all this look like to you, Lige?"

Lige didn't have nothing to say.

"Wes?"

"Well," I said, "I reckon it's jugs."

"Fifty or more, I'd say. Packed inside there nice and tight, with burlap sacking all around. What's in those glass jugs, Wes?"

I sighed. "Corn likker."

"Uhn-huh. Corn likker you boys cooked up over the long winter, using up all your stove wood and spare lumber in the process. You and Lige and old Bryce, who's alive and kicking and tending to his chores this very minute. That about the shape of it?"

"Yes, sir. That's about the shape of it."

"And where were you taking all this corn likker? Wouldn't be over to the reservation to sell to some of the feistier Piegans, would it? Even though it's against the law to sell firewater to Indians?"

"No, sir," I said, "that sure wasn't what we had in mind. We was gonna sell it to the ranchers in Antelope Valley. Charley Hammond and Hank Staggs. . . ."

"Charley Hammond don't drink. He's a Hard Shell Baptist, in case you don't remember. And Hank Staggs don't allow likker of any kind on his property. And Mort Sutherland's got a bad stomach. You figure to sell more'n fifty jugs of corn to Harvey Ames alone? Don't seem likely. Lot more likely you were headed for the reservation, and I reckon the circuit judge'll see it the same when he comes through next week. Meantime, boys, you'll be guests of the county. Close up the evidence and let's get on to town."

We closed her up. Lige said to Conagher: "You knowed, didn't you, Sheriff? Knowed we wasn't taking her to Charley Hammond's, knowed we didn't have old Bryce's remains inside. Knowed all along she was filled up with jugs of corn."

"Well, I had a pretty fair notion."

"How?"

"Funny thing about that outhouse," Conagher said. "When you first rattled to a stop, and again when your horse frog-hopped, I heard noises inside. Good ears is one thing I can brag on, even in cold weather."

"What noises?"

"Sloshing and gurgling. Never yet heard an empty outhouse that sloshed and gurgled. Nor a man's froze-stiff remains that did, either."

Lige punched me in the chest this time. "You and your gol-dang' ideas! You ain't got a lick of sense, Wes Hovey! Ain't got the sense God give a one-eyed grasshopper!"

Well, hell, he didn't neither, did he?

Engines

When Geena moved out and filed for divorce, the first two things I did were to put the house up for sale and to quit Unidyne, a job I'd hated from the beginning. Then I loaded the Jeep and drove straight to Death Valley.

I told no one where I was going. Not that there was anybody to tell, really; we had no close friends, or at least I didn't, and my folks were both dead. Geena could have guessed, of course. She knew me that well, though not nearly well enough to understand my motives.

I did not go to Death Valley because something in my life had died. I went there to start living again.

October is one of the Valley's best months. All months in the Monument are good, as far as I'm concerned, even July and August, when the midday temperatures sometimes exceed 120 degrees Fahrenheit and Death Valley justifies its Paiute Indian name, *Tomesha*—ground afire. If a sere desert climate holds no terrors for you, if you respect it and accept it on its terms, survival is not a problem, and the attractions far outweigh the drawbacks. Still, I'm partial to October, the early part of the month. The beginning of the tourist season is still a month away, temperatures seldom reach 100 degrees, and the constantly changing light show created by sun and wind and clouds is at its most spectacular. You can stay in one place all day, from dawn to dark—Zabriskie Point, say, or the sand dunes near Stovepipe Wells—and with each ten-degree rise and fall of the sun the colors of rock and sand hills change from dark rose to burnished gold, from chocolate brown to purple and indigo and gray-black, with dozens of subtler shades in between.

It had been almost a year since I'd last been to the Valley. Much too long, but it had been a difficult year. I'd been alone on that last visit, as I was alone now, alone the last dozen or so trips since Geena refused to come with me any more five years ago. I preferred it that way. The Valley is a place to be shared only with someone who views it in the same perspective, not as endless miles of coarse, dead landscape but as a vast, almost mystical place—a *living* place—of majestic vistas and stark natural beauty.

Deciding where to go first hadn't been easy. It has more than three thousand square miles, second only among national parks to Yellowstone, and all sorts of terrain; the great trough of the Valley floor with its miles of salt pan two hundred feet and more below sea level, its dunes and alluvial fans, its borate deposits and old borax works, its barren fields of gravel and broken rock, and five enclosing mountain ranges full of hidden cañons, petroglyphs, played-out gold and silver mines, ghost towns. I'd spent an entire evening with my topos—topographical maps put out by the U.S. Geological Survey—and finally settled on the Funeral Mountains and the Chloride Cliffs topo. The Funerals form one of the eastern boundaries, and their foothills and crest not only are laden with a variety of cañons but contain the ruins of the Keane Wonder Mill and mine and the gold boomtown of Chloride City.

I left the Jeep north of Scotty's Castle, near Hells Gate, packed in, and stayed for three days and two nights. The first day was a little rough, even though I'm in good shape. It takes a while to refamiliarize yourself with desert mountain terrain after a year away. The second day was easier. I spent that one exploring Echo Cañon and then tramping among the thick-timbered tramways of the Keane, the decaying mill a mile below it which in the 1890s had twenty stamps processing eighteen hundred tons of ore a month. On the third day I went on up to the Funerals' sheer heights and Chloride City, and the climb neither strained nor winded me.

It was a fine three days. I saw no other people except at a long distance. I reëstablished kinship with the Valley, as only a person who truly loves it can, and all the tension and restless dissatisfaction built up over the past year slowly bled out of me. I could literally feel my spirit reviving, starting to soar again.

I thought about Geena only once, on the morning of the third day as I stood atop one of the crags looking out toward Needles Eye. There was no wind, and the stillness, the utter absence of sound, was so acute it created an almost painful pressure against the eardrums. Of all the things Geena hated about Death Valley, its silence—"void of silence," an early explorer had termed it—topped the list. It terrified her. On our last trip together, when she'd caught me listening, she'd said: "What are you listening *to?* There's nothing to hear in this godforsaken place. It's as if everything has shut down. Not just here, everywhere. As if all the engines have quit working."

She was right, exactly right: as if all the engines have quit working. And that perception, more than anything else, summed up the differences between us. To her, the good things in life, the essence of life itself, were people, cities, constant scurrying activity. She needed to hear the steady, throbbing engines of civilization in order to feel safe, secure, alive. And I needed none of those things, needed *not* to hear the engines.

I remembered something else she'd said to me once, not so long ago. "You're a dreamer, Scott, an unfocused dreamer. Drifting through life looking for something that might not even exist." Well, maybe there was truth in that, too. But if I was looking for something, I had already found part of it right here in Death Valley. And now I could come here as often as I wanted, without restrictions—resigning from Unidyne had seen to that. I couldn't live in the Monument—permanent residence is limited to a small band of Paiutes and Park Service employees—but I could live nearby, in Beatty or Shoshone or one of the other little towns over in the Nevada desert. After the L.A. house sold, I'd be well fixed. And when the money finally did run out, I could hire out as a guide, do odd jobs—whatever it took to support myself. Dreamer with a focus at last.

For a little time, thinking about Geena made me sad. But the Valley is not a place where I can feel sad for long. I had loved her very much at first, when we were both students at UCLA, but over our eleven years together the love had eroded and seeped away, and now what I felt mainly was relief. I was free, and Geena was free. Endings don't have to be painful, not if you look at them as beginnings, instead.

Late that third afternoon I hiked back to where I'd left the Jeep. No one had bothered it; I had never had any trouble with thieves or vandals out here. Before I crawled into my sleeping bag, I sifted through the topos again to pick my next spot. I don't know why I chose the Manly Peak topo. Maybe because I hadn't been in the southern Panamints, through Warm Springs Cañon, in better than three years. Still, it was an odd choice to make. That region was not one of my favorite parts of the Valley. Also, a large portion of the area is under private claim, and the owners of the talc mines along the cañon take a dim view of trespassing: you have to be extra careful to keep to public lands when you pack in there.

In the morning, just before dawn, I ate a couple of nutrition bars for breakfast and then pointed the Jeep down Highway 178. The sun was out by the time I reached the Warm Springs Cañon turn-off. The main road in is unpaved, rutted, and talc-covered, and primarily the domain of eighteen-wheelers passing to and from the mines. You need at least a four-wheel-drive vehicle to negotiate it and the even rougher trails that branch off it. I would not take a passenger car over one inch of that terrain. Neither would anyone else who knows the area or pays attention to the Park Service brochures, guidebooks, and posted signs. That was why I was amazed when I came on the Ford Taurus.

I had turned off the main cañon road ten miles in, onto the trail into Butte Valley, and, when I rounded a turn on the washboard surface, there it was, pulled off into the shadow of a limestone shelf. The left rear tire was flat, and a stain that had spread out from underneath told me the oil pan was ruptured. No one was visible inside or anywhere in the immediate vicinity.

I brought the Jeep up behind and went to have a look. The Ford had been there a while—that was clear. At least two days. The look and feel of the oil stain proved that. I had to be the first to come by since its abandonment, or it wouldn't still be sitting here like this. Not many hikers or off-roaders venture out this way in the off season; the big ore trucks use the main cañon road, and there aren't enough park rangers for daily back-country patrols.

The Ford's side windows were so dust- and talc-caked that I could barely see through them. I tried the driver's door; it was unlocked. The interior was empty except for two things on the front seat. One was a woman's purse, open, the edge of a wallet poking out. The other was a piece of lined notepaper with writing on it in felt-tip pen, held down by the weight of the purse.

I slid the paper free. Date on top—two days ago—and below that—"To Frank Spicer,"—followed by several lines of shaky, black, hand printing. I sensed what it was even before I finished reading the words.

189

I have no hope left. You and Conners have seen to that. I can't fight you any more and I can't go on not knowing if Kevin is safe, how you must be poisoning his mind even if you haven't hurt him physically. Someday he'll find out what kind of man you really are. Someday he _will_ find out. And I pray to God he makes you pay for what you've done.

I love you, Kevin. God forgive me.

I couldn't quite decipher the scrawled signature. Christine, or Christina something—not Spicer. I opened the wallet and fanned through the card section until I found her driver's license. The Ford had California plates, and the license had also been issued in this state. Christina Dunbar. Age 32. San Diego address. The face in the ID photo was slender and fair-haired and unsmiling.

The wallet contained one other photo, of a nice-looking boy eight or nine years old—a candid shot taken at a lake or large river. Kevin? Nothing else in the wallet told me anything. One credit card was all she owned. And twelve dollars in fives and singles.

I returned the wallet to the purse, folded the note in there with it. In my mouth was a dryness that had nothing to do with the day's gathering heat. And in my mind was a feeling of urgency much more intense than the situation called for. If she'd brought along a gun or pills or some other lethal device, she was long dead by now. If she'd wanted the Valley to do the job for her, plenty enough time had elapsed for that, too, given the perilous terrain and the proliferation of sidewinders and daytime temperatures in the mid-nineties and no water and improper clothing. Yet there was a chance she was still alive. A chance I could keep her that way, if I could find her.

I tossed her purse into the Jeep, uncased my 7x50 Zeiss

binoculars, and climbed up on the hood to scan the surrounding terrain. The Valley floor here was flattish, mostly
fields of fractured rock slashed by shallow washes. Clumps of
low-growing creosote bush and turtleback were the only vegetation. I had a fairly good look over a radius of several hundred yards—no sign of her.

Some distance ahead there was higher ground. I drove too
fast on the rough road, had to force myself to slow down. At
the top of a rise I stopped again, climbed a jut of limestone to a
notch in its crest. From there I had a much wider view, all the
way to Striped Butte and the lower reaches of the Panamints.

The odds were against my spotting her, even with the
powerful Zeiss glasses. The topography's rumpled irregu-
larity created too many hidden places; she might have wandered miles in any direction. But I did locate her, and in less
than ten minutes, and, when I did, I felt no surprise. It was as
if at some deep level I'd been certain all along that I would.

She was a quarter of a mile away, to the southwest, at the
bottom of a salt-streaked wash. Lying on her side, motionless, knees drawn up to her chest, face and part of her blonde
head hidden in the crook of one bare arm. It was impossible
to tell at this distance if she were alive or dead.

The wash ran down out of the foothills like a long, twisted
scar, close to the trail for some distance, then hooking away
from it in a gradual snake-track curve. Where she lay was at
least four hundred yards from the four-wheel track. I picked
out a trail landmark roughly opposite, then scrambled back
down to the Jeep.

It took me more than an hour to get to her: drive to the
landmark, load my pack with two extra soft-plastic water bottles and the first-aid kit, strap the pack on, and then hike
across humps and flats of broken rock as loose and treach-
erous as talus. Even though the pre-noon temperature was

still in the eighties, I was sweating heavily—and I'd used up a pint of water to replace the sweat loss, by the time I reached the wash.

She still lay in the same drawn-up position. And she didn't stir at the noises I made, the clatter of dislodged rocks, as I slid down the wash's bank. I went to one knee beside her, groped for a sunburned wrist. Pulse, faint and irregular. I did not realize until then that I had been holding my breath; I let it out thin and hissing between my teeth.

She wore only a thin, short-sleeved shirt, a pair of Levi's, and tattered Reeboks. The exposed areas of her skin were burned raw, coated with salt from dried sweat that was as gritty as fine sand; the top of her scalp was flecked with dried blood from ruptured blisters. I saw no snake or scorpion bites, no limb fractures or swellings. But she was badly dehydrated. At somewhere between fifteen percent and twenty-two percent dehydration, a human being will die, and she was at, or near, the danger zone.

Gently I took hold of her shoulders, eased her over onto her back. Her limbs twitched; she made a little whimpering sound. She was on the edge of consciousness, more submerged than not. The sun's white glare hurt her eyes even through the tightly closed lids. She turned her head, lifted an arm painfully across the bridge of her nose.

I freed one of the foil-wrapped water bottles, slipped off the attached cap. Her lips were cracked, split deeply in a couple of places; I dribbled water on them, to get her to open them. Then I eased the spout into her mouth and squeezed out a few more drops.

At first she struggled, twisting her head, moaning deep in her throat: the part of her that wanted death rebelling against revival and awareness. But her will to live hadn't completely deserted her, and her thirst was too acute. She swallowed some of the warm liquid, swallowed more when I lifted her head and held it cushioned against my knee. Before long she was sucking greedily at the spout, like an infant at its mother's nipple. Her hands came up and clutched at the bottle; I let her take it away from me, let her drain it. The idea of parceling out water to a dehydration victim is a fallacy. You have to saturate the parched tissues as fast as possible to accelerate the restoration of normal functions.

I opened another bottle, raised her to a sitting position, and then gave it to her. Shelter was the next most important thing. I took the lightweight space blanket from my pack, unfolded it, and shook it out. A space blanket is five by seven feet, coated on one side with a filler of silver insulating material and reflective surface. Near where she lay, behind her to the east, I hand-scraped a sandy area free of rocks. Then I set up the blanket into a lean-to, using take-down tent poles to support the front edge and tying them off with nylon cord to rocks placed at a forty-five-degree angle from the shelter corners. I secured the ground side of the lean-to with more rocks and sand atop the blanket's edge.

Christina Dunbar was sitting slumped forward when I finished, her head cradled in her hands. The second water bottle, as empty as the first, lay beside her. I gripped her shoulders again, and this time she stiffened, fought me weakly as I drew her backward and pressed her down into the lean-to's shade. The struggles stopped when I pillowed her head with the pack. She lay still, half on her side, her eyes still squeezed tight shut. Conscious now but not ready to face either me or the fact that she was still alive.

The first-aid kit contained a tube of Neosporin. I said as I uncapped it: "I've got some burn medicine here. I'm going to rub it on your face and scalp first."

She made a throat sound that might have been a protest.

But when I squeezed out some of the ointment and began to smooth it over her blistered skin, she remained passive. Lay there, silent and rigid, as I ministered to her.

I used the entire tube of Neosporin, most of it on her face and arms. None of the cuts and abrasions she'd suffered was serious; the medicine would disinfect those, too. There was nothing I could do for the bruises on her upper arms, along her jaw, and on the left temple. I wondered where she'd got them. Not stumbling around in the desert: they were more than two days old, already fading.

When I was done, I opened another quart of water, took a nutrition bar from my pack. Her eyes were open when I looked at her again. Gray-blue, dull with pain and exhaustion, staring fixedly at me without blinking. Hating me a little, I thought.

I said—"Take some more water."—and extended the bottle to her.

"No."

"Still thirsty, aren't you?"

"No."

"We both know you are."

"Who're you?" Her voice was as dry and cracked as her lips, but strong enough. "How'd you find me?"

"Scott Davis. I was lucky. So are you."

"Lucky," she said.

"Drink the water, Christina."

"How do you know . . . ? Oh."

"That's right. I read the note."

"Why couldn't you just let me die? Why did you have to come along and find me?"

"Drink."

I held the bottle out close to her face. Her eyes shifted to it; the tip of her tongue flicked out, snake-like, as if she were tasting the water. Then, grimacing, she lifted onto an elbow and took the bottle with an angry, swiping gesture —anger directed at herself, not me, as if for an act of self-betrayal. She drank almost half of it, coughed, and then lowered the bottle.

"Go a little slower with the rest of it."

"Leave me alone."

"I can't do that, Christina."

"I want to sleep."

"No, you don't." I unwrapped the nutrition bar. "Eat as much of this as you can get down. Slowly, little bites."

She shook her head, holding her arms, stiff and tight, against her sides.

"Please," I said.

"I don't want any food."

"Your body needs the nourishment."

"No."

"I'll force-feed you if I have to."

She held out a little longer, but her eyes were on the bar the entire time. When she finally took it, it was with the same gesture of self-loathing. Her first few bites were nibbles, but the honey taste revived her hunger, and she went at the bar the way she had at the water bottle. She almost choked on the first big chunk she tried to swallow. I made her slow down, sip water between each bite.

"How do you feel?" I asked when she was finished.

"Like I'm going to live, damn you."

"Good. We'll stay here for a while, until you're strong enough to walk."

"Walk where?"

"My Jeep, over on the trail. Four hundred yards or so, and the terrain is pretty rough. I don't want to have to carry you, at least not the whole way."

"Then what?"

"You need medical attention. There's an infirmary at Furnace Creek."

"And after that, the psycho ward," she said, but not as if she cared. "Where's the nearest one?"

I let that pass. "If you feel up to talking," I said, "I'm a good listener."

"About what?"

"Why you did this to yourself."

"Tried to kill myself, you mean. Commit suicide."

"All right. Why, Christina?"

"You read my note."

"It's pretty vague. Is Kevin your son?"

She winced when I spoke the name. Turned her head away without answering.

I didn't press it. Instead, I shifted around and lay back on my elbows, with my upper body in the lean-to's shade. I was careful not to touch her. It was another windless day, and the near-noon stillness was as complete as it had been the other morning in the Funerals. For a time nothing moved anywhere; then a chuckwalla lizard scurried up the bank of the wash, followed a few seconds later by a horned toad. It looked as though the toad were chasing the lizard, but like so many things in the Valley that was illusion. Toads and lizards are not enemies.

It was not long before Christina stirred and said: "Is there any more water?" Her tone had changed; there was resignation in it now, as if she had accepted, at least for the time being, the burden of remaining alive.

I sat up, took one of the last two full quarts from my pack. "Make this the last until we're ready to leave," I said as I handed it to her. "It's a long walk to the Jeep, and we'll have to share the last bottle."

She nodded, drank less thirstily, and lowered the bottle

with it still two-thirds full. That was a good sign. Her body was responding, its movements stronger and giving her less pain.

I let her have another energy bar. She took it without argument, ate it slowly with sips of water. Then she lifted herself into a sitting position, her head not quite touching the slant of the blanket. She was just a few inches over five feet, thin but wiry. The kind of body she had and the fact that she'd taken care of it was a major reason for her survival and swift recovery.

She said: "I guess you might as well know."

"If you want to tell me."

"Kevin's my son. Kevin Andrew Spicer. He'll be ten years old in December."

"Frank Spicer is your ex-husband?"

"Yes, and I hope his soul rots in hell."

"Custody battle?"

"Oh, yes, there was a custody battle. But I won. I had full legal custody of my son."

"Had?"

"Frank kidnapped him."

"You mean literally?"

"Literally."

"When?"

"A year and a half ago," Christina said. "He had visitation rights, every other weekend. He picked Kevin up one Friday afternoon and never brought him back. I haven't seen either of them since."

"The authorities couldn't find them?"

"Nobody could find them. Not the police, not the FBI, not any of the three private detectives I hired. I think they're still somewhere in the Southwest . . . Nevada or Arizona or New Mexico. But I don't know. I don't know."

"How could they vanish so completely?"

"Money. Everything comes down to money."

"Not everything."

"He was a successful commercial artist. And bitter because he felt he was prostituting his great talent. Even after the settlement he had a net worth of more than two hundred thousand dollars."

"He liquidated all his assets before he took Kevin?"

"Every penny."

"He must've wanted the boy very badly."

"He did, but not because he loves him."

"To get back at you?"

"To hurt me. He hates me."

"Why? The custody battle?"

"That, and because I divorced him. He can't stand to lose any of his possessions."

"He sounds unstable."

"Unstable is a polite term for it. Frank Spicer is a paranoid sociopath with delusions of grandeur. That's what a psychiatrist I talked to called him."

"Abusive?"

"Not at first. Not until he started believing I was sleeping with everybody from the mayor to the mailman. I was never unfaithful to him, not once."

"Did he abuse Kevin, too?"

"No, thank God. He never touched Kevin. At least . . . not before he took him away from me."

"You think he may have harmed the boy since?"

"He's capable of it. He's capable of anything. There's no doubt of that now."

"Now?"

Head shake. She drank more water.

"Conners," I said. "Who's he?"

She winced again. "The last straw."

I waited, but she didn't go on. She was not ready to talk about Conners yet.

"Christina, why did you come here?"

"I don't know. I was on the main road, and there was a sign. . . ."

"I mean Death Valley itself. All the way from San Diego, nearly four hundred miles."

"I didn't drive here from San Diego."

"Isn't that where you live?"

"Yes, but I was in Las Vegas. I came from there."

"Why were you in Vegas?"

"Fool's errand," she said bitterly.

"Something happened there. What was it?"

She didn't answer. For more than a minute she sat stiffly, squinting in the direction of Striped Butte; the sun on its anamorphic conglomeration of ribbons of crinold limestone, jasper, and other minerals was dazzling. Then. . . .

"A man called me a few days ago. He said his name was Conners, and he knew where Frank and Kevin were living, but he wanted a thousand dollars for the information. In cash, delivered to him in Vegas."

"Did you know him?"

"No."

"But you believed him."

"I wanted to believe him," she said. "He claimed to've known Frank years ago, to've had business dealings with him. He mentioned the names of people I knew. And the last detective I hired . . . he traced Frank and Kevin to a Vegas suburb six weeks ago. They disappeared again the day after he found out where they'd been staying."

"Why didn't you send the detective to meet with Conners?"

199

"He stopped working for me a month ago, when I couldn't pay him any more. All the settlement money was gone, and I had nothing left to sell. And no friends left to borrow from."

"Then you couldn't raise the thousand Conners demanded?"

"No. I couldn't raise it. So I stole it."

I didn't say anything.

"I was desperate," she said. "Desperate and crazy."

"Where did you steal it?"

"From the hardware supply company where I work . . . worked. My boss is a nice guy. He loaned me money twice before, he was supportive and sympathetic, but he just couldn't loan me any more, he said. So I paid him back by taking a thousand dollars out of the company account. Easy . . . I was office manager. Then I drove to Vegas and gave it to Conners."

"And it was all just a scam," I said. "He didn't know where Spicer and Kevin are."

"Oh, he knew, all right. He knew because Frank had set the whole thing up. That was part of the message Conners delivered afterward."

"Afterward?"

"After he beat me up and raped me."

"Jesus," I said.

"Frank is tired of being dogged by detectives. Frank says I'd better leave him and Kevin alone from now on. Frank says, if I don't, there'll be more of the same, only next time he'll do it himself, and it won't just be rape and a beating . . . he'll kill me. End of message."

"Did you call the police?"

"What for? Conners isn't his real name, and he doesn't live in Vegas. What could the police have done except maybe arrest me and send me back to San Diego to stand trial for theft? No. No. I stayed in the motel room where it happened until I felt well enough to leave, and then I started driving. By the time the car quit on me, I was way out here in the middle of nowhere, and I didn't care any more. I just didn't want to go on living."

"You still feel that way?"

"What do you think?"

I said: "There are a lot of miles between Vegas and Death Valley. And a lot of remote desert. Why did you come this far?"

"I don't know. I just kept driving, that's all."

"Have you ever been to the Valley before?"

"No."

"Was it on your mind? Death Valley, dead place, place to go and die?"

"No. I didn't even know where I was until I saw a sign. What difference does it make?"

"It makes a difference. I think it does."

"Well, I don't. The only thing that matters is that you found me before it was too late."

She picked up the water bottle, sat holding it in brooding silence without drinking. I gave my attention to the Panamints, Manly Peak and the taller, hazy escarpments of Telescope Peak to the north. To some they were silent and brooding—bare monoliths of dark-gray basalt and limestone, like tombstones towering above a vast graveyard. But not to me. I saw them as old and benevolent guardians, comforting in their size and age and austerity. Nurturing. The Paiutes believe that little mountain spirits, *Kai-nu-suvs,* live deep in their rock recesses—kindly spirits. as beautiful as sunset clouds and as pure as fresh snow. When clouds mass above the peaks, the *Kai-nu-suvs* ride deer and bighorn sheep, driving their charges in wild rides among the crags. For such joyous celebrations of life, the Paiutes cherish them.

Time passed. I sat looking and listening. Mostly listening, until I grew aware of heat rays against my hands where they rested flat on my thighs. The sun had reached and passed its zenith, was robbing the shelter of its shade. If we didn't leave soon, I would have to reset the position of the lean-to.

"How do you feel?" I asked Christina. "Strong enough to try walking?"

She was still resigned. "I can try," she said.

"Stay where you are for a couple of minutes, while I get ready. I'll work around you."

I gathered and stowed the empty water bottles, took down the lean-to, and stowed the stakes and then strapped on the pack. When I helped Christina to her feet, she seemed able to stand all right without leaning on me. I shook out the blanket, draped it over her head and shoulders so that her arms were covered, showed her how to hold it in place under her chin. Then I slipped an arm around her thin body, and we set out.

It was a long slow trek to the Jeep. And a painful one for her, though she didn't complain, didn't speak the entire time. We stayed in the wash most of the way, despite the fact that it added a third as much distance, because the footing was easier for her. I stopped frequently so she could rest; and I let her have almost all the remaining water. Still, by the time we reached the trail her legs were wobbly, and most of her new-gained strength was gone. I had to swing her up and carry her the last two hundred yards. But it was not much of a strain. She was like a child in my arms.

I eased her into the passenger seat, took the blanket, and put it and my pack into the rear. There were two quarts of water left back there. I drank from one, two long swallows, before I slid in under the wheel. She had slumped down limply on the other seat, with her head back and her eyes shut. Her breath came and went in ragged little pants.

"Christina?"

"I'm awake," she said.

"Here. More water."

She drank without opening her eyes.

I said: "There are some things I want to say before we go. Something important that needs to be settled."

"What would that be?"

"When we get to Furnace Creek, I'm not going to report you as an attempted suicide. We'll say you made the mistake of driving out here in a passenger car, and, when it broke down, you tried to walk out and lost your sense of direction. That sort of thing happens a dozen times a year in the Valley. The rangers won't think anything of it."

"Why bother? It doesn't matter if you report me as a psycho case."

"You're not a psycho case. And it does matter. I want to keep on helping you."

"There's nothing you can do for me."

"I can help you find your son."

Her head jerked up; she opened her eyes to stare at me. "What're you talking about?"

"Just what I said. I want to help you find your son and take him back from his father."

"You can't be serious."

"I've never been more serious."

"But why would you . . . ?"

"A lot of reasons. Because you're still alive and I'd like you to stay that way. Because I don't want Frank Spicer to get away with kidnapping Kevin or with having you raped and beaten. Because it's right. Because I can."

She shook her head—trying to shake away disbelief so she could cling to hope again. "The heat must have made you crazy. I told you. I'm a fugitive. I stole money from my boss in San Diego. . . ."

"You also told me he was supportive and sympathetic. Chances are he still is, or will be if he gets his thousand dollars back. I'll call him tonight, explain the situation, offer to send him the money right away if he drops any charges he may have filed. With interest, if he asks for it."

"My God, you'd do that?"

"You can pay me back after we find Kevin. Money's not a problem, Christina. I have more than enough for both of us."

"But Frank . . . you don't know him. He meant what he said about killing me. He'd kill you, too."

"He won't harm either of us. I'll see to that. Or Kevin, if I can help it. I'm not afraid of men like Frank Spicer. He may be disturbed, but he's also a coward. Sending Conners proves that."

Another head shake. "How could we hope to find them? The FBI couldn't in a year and a half, the detectives couldn't. . . ."

"They didn't spend all their time looking," I said. "You and I can, as long as it takes. Time's not a problem, either. Before I came out here my wife filed for divorce, and I quit my job. That part of my life is over. There's nothing to keep me from spending the rest of it any way I see fit."

"Why *this* way? Why would you do so much for a stranger? What do you expect to get out of it?"

"Nothing from you, Christina. It's as much for myself as it is for you."

"I want to believe you, but I just . . . I don't understand. Are you trying to be some kind of hero?"

"There's nothing heroic about me. My wife once called me an unfocused dreamer, drifting through life looking for something that might not even exist. She was half right. What

I've been looking for I've had all along without realizing it . . . Death Valley, and my relationship to it. I've been coming here ever since I was a kid, more than twenty years, and I've always felt that it's a living place, not a dead one. Now . . . it seems almost sentient to me. As if it were responsible for bringing us together. I could have gone anywhere in three thousand square miles today, and I came to the exact spot you did two days ago. I could easily have missed finding you, but I didn't. The feeling of sentience is illusion, I suppose, but that doesn't make it any less important. If I don't finish saving your life . . . help you find your son, give you a reason to go on living . . . then none of what's happened today will mean anything. And my relationship with the Valley will never be the same again. Does that make any sense to you?"

"Maybe," she said slowly. "Maybe it does."

"Will you let me finish what's been started, then? For your son's sake, if not for yours or mine?"

She had no words yet. Her head turned away from me, and at first I thought she was staring out through the windshield. Then some of the hurt smoothed out of her ravaged face, and her expression grew almost rapt, and I knew she wasn't looking at anything. Knew, too, what her answer would be. And that there was a closer bond between us than I'd thought.

She was listening.

What are you listening to? There's nothing to hear in this god-forsaken place.

Yes, there was. Geena just hadn't been able to hear it.

It's as if everything has shut down. Not just here, everywhere. As if all the engines have quit working.

No, not all. There was still one engine you could hear if you tried hard enough. The engine I'd been listening to out in the wash, when I'd been making up my mind about Christina and Kevin and Frank Spicer. The engine she was listening to now. One engine clear and steady in the void of silence, the only one that really counts.

Your own.

About the Author

Bill Pronzini was born in Petaluma, California. His earliest Western fiction was the short story, "Sawtooth Justice," published in *Zane Grey Western Magazine* (11/69). A number of short stories followed before he published his first Western novel, THE GALLOWS LAND (1983), which has the same beginning as the story, "Decision," but with the rider, instead, returning to the Todd ranch. Although Pronzini has earned an enviable reputation as an author of detective stories, he has continued periodically to write Western novels, most notably perhaps STARVATION CAMP (1984) and FIREWIND (1989) as well as Western short stories. Over the years he has also edited a great number of Western fiction anthologies and single-author Western story collections. Most recently these have included UNDER THE BURNING SUN: WESTERN STORIES (Five Star Westerns, 1997) by H.A. DeRosso, RENEGADE RIVER: WESTERN STORIES (Five Star Westerns, 1998) by Giff Cheshire, RIDERS OF THE SHADOWLANDS: WESTERN STORIES (Five Star Westerns, 1999) by H.A. DeRosso, and HEADING WEST: WESTERN STORIES (Five Star Westerns, 1999) by Noel M. Loomis. In his own Western stories, Pronzini has tended toward narratives that avoid excessive violence and, instead, are character studies in which a person has to deal with personal flaws or learn to live with the consequences of previous actions. As an editor and anthologist, Pronzini has demonstrated both rare *éclat* and reliable good taste in selecting very fine stories by other authors, fiction notable for its human drama and memorable characters. He is married to author

Marcia Muller, who has written Western stories as well as detective stories, and even occasionally collaborated with her husband on detective novels. They make their home in Petaluma, California. TRACKS IN THE SAND: WESTERN STORIES by H.A. DeRosso edited by Bill Pronzini will be his next Five Star Western.

Acknowledgments

"All the Long Years" first appeared in WESTERYEAR (Evans, 1988) edited by Ed Gorman. Copyright © 1988 by Bill Pronzini.

"Lady One-Eye" first appeared in *Louis L'Amour Western Magazine* (9/94). Copyright © 1994 by Bill Pronzini.

"Hero" first appeared in SMALL FELONIES (SMP, 1988) by Bill Pronzini. Copyright © 1988 by Bill Pronzini.

"Doc Christmas, Painless Dentist" first appeared in *Louis L'Amour Western Magazine* (5/94). Copyright © 1994 by Bill Pronzini.

"McIntosh's Chute" by Jack Foxx first appeared in NEW FRONTIERS: VOLUME ONE (Tor, 1990) edited by Martin H. Greenberg and Bill Pronzini. Copyright © 1989 by Bill Pronzini.

"Fyfe and the Drummers" first appeared in NEW FRONTIERS: VOLUME TWO (Tor, 1990) edited by Martin H. Greenberg and Bill Pronzini. Copyright © 1990 by Bill Pronzini.

"Markers" first appeared in ROUNDUP (Doubleday, 1982) edited by Stephen Overholser. Copyright © 1982 by the Western Writers of America, Inc.

" 'Give-A-Damn' Jones" first appeared in THE FIRST FIVE STAR WESTERN CORRAL (Five Star Westerns, 2000) edited by Jon Tuska and Vicki Piekarski. Copyright © 2000 by Bill Pronzini.

"The Gambler" first appeared in NEW FRONTIERS: VOLUME ONE (Tor, 1990) edited by Martin H. Greenberg and Bill Pronzini. Copyright © 1989 by Bill Pronzini.

"Wooden Indian" first appeared in *Alfred Hitchcock's Mystery Magazine* (3/89). Copyright © 1989 by Davis Publications, Inc.

"Decision" first appeared as "I'll See to Your Horse" in *Zane Grey Western Magazine* (2/72). It was later rewritten and in-